"Well, Miss Darr, I believe the time has come for us to discuss business. I am prepared to give you ten thousand dollars in cash today. In return, I would like three favors. Number one, you must learn the music that is in this envelope. Number two, you must be available to travel to a major European city between November fourth and November ninth of this year. And number three, you must tell absolutely no one about this transaction. Will you accept?"

"Why does it have to remain a secret?"

"Unfortunately, I cannot tell you. But at the first sign of any impropriety on our part you may withdraw and the money will remain yours . . ."

What the man didn't mention, though, was what would happen if Judith Darr did anything improper . . .

THE Beethoven CONSPIRACY

THE Beethoven CONSPIRACY

THOMAS HAUSER

A TOM DOHERTY ASSOCIATES BOOK

THE BEETHOVEN CONSPIRACY

The author gratefully acknowledges permission to quote the following material:
   Excerpts on pages 141 to 143, from *Letters of Beethoven*, edited and translated by Emily Anderson, published by Macmillan & Co., Ltd., London and Basingstoke, 1961.
   Excerpts on pages 167 to 168, from *Beethoven As I Knew Him: A Biography* by Anton Felix Schindler, edited by Donald W. MacArdle and translated by Constance S. Jolly. Copyright 1966 Mrs. Ruth W. MacArdle, published by Faber and Faber Ltd, London, and The University of North Carolina Press, Chapel Hill.

Reprinted by arrangement with Macmillan Publishing Company

A TOR Book

Published by Tom Doherty Associates
49 West 24 Street
New York, N.Y. 10010

First TOR printing: December 1985

ISBN: 0-812-50451-8
CAN. ED.: 0-812-50452-6

Printed in the United States of America

For Robin and Bill

Acknowledgments

The Beethoven Conspiracy was written with the help of many people. Marcy Rosen, Kim Kashkashian, Sheryl Henze, Tina Pelikan, and Larry Dutton are musicians who gave generously of their time and knowledge. Jacques Français enlightened me on the subject of rare string instruments, and Kathy Erlandson of the New York Philharmonic opened many doors. Robert Philios, Frank Nicolosi, Jim Ferguson, and Warren Tyranski—all of the New York City Police Department—provided invaluable technical assistance. Eleanor Leslie and Peter Georgas were instrumental in arranging for on-site research in Vienna and Salzburg. As always, I relied on family members and special friends for encouragement and support.

In addition, I am deeply indebted to David Branson and Robert Berger for their wise counsel and help.

Prologue

THE DUSK WAS COLD. March snow had fallen. For three days, the great man had lain unconscious, his still-powerful lungs breathing an ominous death rattle that defied the dissolution of his ravaged frame. His pock-marked face was whitish gray, with burning eyes that lay shuttered beneath a broad forehead and unkempt hair. His liver, a crude autopsy later revealed, was covered with bean-sized nodules, greenish blue in color, shrunk to half its proper size. His long-useless auditory nerves were withered and dry, the arteries that paralleled them thick and cartilaginous.

As night approached, a raging storm obscured the sky. Thunder rolled. A flash of lightning lit up the heavens, bathing the death chamber in a garish, other-worldly glow. At the flash, the great man opened his eyes and lifted his hand in a tightly clenched fist, raging defiantly against the Gods—then fell back, dead.

Von Breuning and Schindler arrived moments later.

It had begun.

Tentatively, because she wasn't in the habit of accepting invitations from strangers, Judith opened the door and stepped inside. The restaurant was quiet and gently lit, well air-conditioned against the mid-day summer heat, elegant, comfortable. The south-wall windows looked out onto a shady tree-lined street on Manhattan's Upper West Side.

When her eyes had adjusted to the indoor light, Judith searched for some sign of her host. Three or four couples were seated at tables around the room, all of them dressed more fashionably than she was. She tugged anxiously at the rough hemp belt on her blue cotton skirt and thought back to the voice that had addressed her on the telephone little more than an hour ago:

"Miss Darr?"

"Yes."

"My name is Klaus Ehrlich. I'm a great admirer

of your music. I wonder if it would be possible for us to meet to discuss a business proposition?''

''Who are you?''

''I have just told you. My name is Klaus Ehrlich. The business I wish to discuss involves a performance in Europe. Perhaps we could meet this afternoon for lunch.''

The tables were covered with white linen cloths, a small crystal vase with roses and lilies centered on each. The walls were lined with Renoir-like murals depicting nubile women frolicking in a bucolic autumn setting. Sitting alone in a corner, his back to the wall, a conservatively dressed man beckoned. Judith approached and he rose to greet her.

''Miss Darr. I'm Klaus Ehrlich. It was good of you to come.''

Judith sat, and began making mental notes. Ehrlich was tall and thin, with light brown hair streaked silvery gray. He wore gold-rimmed glasses, and spoke with a definite German accent.

''Would you care for a cocktail?''

She shook her head, and he offered the menu instead. They ordered. Ehrlich resumed the conversation after the waiter had left.

''Miss Darr, this is indeed a pleasure. But, in truth, I know very little about you. I know that you are twenty-six years old, that you were born in Vermont, and that you are an exceptionally gifted violist. Perhaps you could tell me, when did you first take up the instrument?''

Judith eyed her host warily. ''I thought we were

here to discuss business,'' she wanted to answer—
wanted, but didn't. She wasn't very experienced at
this sort of thing, and business deals probably began
with small talk.

"I was seven," she answered. "The year before,
I'd asked my parents if I could take piano lessons and
they said yes. I played for about a year—one lesson a
week, plus half an hour a day for practice. Then,
about a year later, I sat in on a viola lesson my
teacher was giving one of her other students. Right
away, I fell in love with the instrument.''

"Certainly, you must be very pleased with the
manner in which your playing has progressed.''

"Overall, I'm happy with it.''

Maybe Ehrlich was some sort of weirdo and the
entire lunch was a sexual come-on. He'd seen her
perform, gotten off on her body, and found her number in the Manhattan telephone directory. That was
the problem with having a listed number. Still, they
were in a restaurant surrounded by other patrons. He
couldn't do very much.

The waiter returned with "pâté for the gentleman,
cream of leek soup for the young lady.''

"No doubt, Miss Darr, you're aware of your talent. Everyone recognizes that you have a brilliant
future.''

Flattered, flustered, annoyed, on edge, Judith fingered the wicker basket of thick warm bread on the
table between them. Each moment made it less likely
that she'd enjoy her lunch. Ehrlich was stiff and
much too formal. Everything seemed awkward and

out of place. And then something extraordinary happened. Klaus Ehrlich began to talk—about music. And very quickly it became apparent that he knew more about his subject (which happened to be the all-consuming passion in Judith's life) than any person she'd ever met. Professor, student, artist, scholar—he seemed to be all those things rolled into one. Enchanted, Judith listened as he talked. At times, his tone was a bit pedantic. There were moments when he spoke so slowly, giving such consideration to each detail, that she wished he'd skip a word and hurry on so that she could hear the rest. But instinctively she knew he was far too thorough and too much in love with his subject to gloss over any facet of it. So she contented herself with listening. And with incredible appreciation, understanding, and love, he continued to talk.

The meal lasted two hours. When it was done, Ehrlich folded his napkin in a neat triangular pattern and, ever so slightly, his voice dropped.

"Well, Miss Darr, this has been an absolute delight. But now, I believe, the time has come for us to discuss business." Reaching into his jacket, he drew out a plain white envelope. "Miss Darr, I am prepared to give you ten thousand dollars in cash today. In return, I would like three favors. Number one, you must learn the music that is in this envelope. Number two, you must be available to travel to a major European city between the days of November fourth and November ninth of this year. And number three, you must tell absolutely no one about this transaction. Will you accept?''

Bewildered, Judith stared at her host. "I don't understand."

"I believe the terms are clear enough. What is it that you do not understand?"

"Everything—the money, the music. Who are you?"

"I have told you. My name is Klaus Ehrlich. Beyond that, I am an inconsequential figure. You would not be interested in my life."

"But I am."

"Were I so inclined, I could make up a history to satisfy your curiosity. But that wouldn't be honest, and I want to be completely honest with you."

Just for a moment, they measured each other.

"Why me?"

"Because you are a young woman with considerable talent."

"How many other people have you involved in this project?"

"That should be of no concern to you."

"But there are others?"

"Yes."

"Why does it have to remain a secret?"

"This, unfortunately, I cannot explain. I will simply tell you that I am in the employ of an honorable man, and there is nothing unlawful or improper about what we ask of you. Should you accept, at the first sign of any impropriety you may withdraw and the ten thousand dollars will remain yours. As you are aware, ten thousand dollars is a considerable sum of money.''

All of the emotion that had accompanied the talk of music was gone from his voice. Every word was coldly and mechanically spoken.

"If I accept, where would I be going those days in November?"

"To a major European city."

"For some type of performance?"

"That is correct. Prior to departure, you will be notified as to the exact location and given a fully paid airplane ticket. Your accommodations will be single room and deluxe. For your efforts, you will receive the advance sum of ten thousand dollars. All I ask is that you learn the music in this envelope, make yourself available from November four through November nine, and tell absolutely no one about our arrangement."

"Can I see the music?"

"Only if you accept."

"Who wrote it?"

"That is unimportant."

"Why should I trust you?"

For the first time since their discussion of business had begun, Ehrlich smiled. "Miss Darr, that is a question *I* should ask, not you. I am about to give you ten thousand dollars without even a written receipt. It is I who must trust."

Ten thousand dollars! Okay, Judith, get hold of yourself! Her thoughts were spinning. Ten thousand dollars! That was as much money as she made in an entire year of scrounging for quartet performances, giving lessons, and subbing for the New York Philharmonic. Ten thousand dollars for one week's work, from a man who knew and loved music. With Europe thrown in the bargain to boot.

"Miss Darr, will you join us?"

"I don't know. I need time to think."

"Very well. For the moment, please tell absolutely no one about our discussion. I will call for your answer in twenty-four hours."

Like athletes, cops grow old before their time. Doctors, lawyers, politicians—they're just beginning to peak at forty. Cops at forty are over the hill, tired, ready to retire.

Richard Marritt was forty-four. For nineteen years, he'd been a cop, the last seven as a detective on Manhattan's Upper West Side. In twelve months, he'd be eligible to retire on a full pension. His wife was forty-two and putting on weight. "Well-rounded, it's more feminine in an older woman" was what he told her; but he wished she'd take off the extra pounds. Together, they'd had two children. For a while, it looked as though there'd be a third. The abortion, two years ago, still bothered him. Every now and then it would pop up in his thoughts, usually when he was remembering how the kids (now eight and ten) had learned to walk and talk.

Marritt wasn't good-looking. He was five-foot-ten

and on the heavy side. His black hair was still thick and, for someone his age, there was little gray. "Plodding" was a word that a lot of people used to describe him. "Plodding" and "decent" and "a good cop." Like most cops, he hated the unpredictable. He also hated the subway, but he rode it daily because it was the fastest, cheapest way to get to work. Now, as he made his way home to Queens on a graffiti-lined car with three other passengers, his mind was locked on a favorite fantasy: Richard Marritt—in the twilight of his career as the premiere baseball player in America. Reggie Jackson might hit the ball farther. Dave Parker had a better throwing arm and glove. But for twenty-two years, Richard Marritt had been the big league's Rock of Gibraltar, playing first base for the New York Yankees. Twenty-two years, twelve batting titles, four Most Valuable Player awards. He'd been on fourteen pennant winners and eleven World Series champions; the purest natural hitter since Ted Williams; nineteen seasons with over 200 hits; a lifetime batting average of .334. And now, in August of his final season, Marritt needed just 27 more base hits to surpass the immortal Ty Cobb.

The train stopped at Queens Plaza, and a blast of music assaulted Marritt's senses. He looked up as a macho-looking white guy boogied into the car. They exchanged glances: Marritt, in his rumpled sixty-dollar gray suit; the other guy, maybe twenty years old, hair slicked back, wearing a thick gold chain around his neck, carrying a big cassette tape recorder that was booming all over the place.

"It's been a long day," Marritt told himself. "I have a headache, and all I want is to go home."

Ninety percent of the seats in the subway car were empty. The macho white guy sat ten inches from Marritt. To compensate for the roar of the subway, he turned the music louder.

Ten seconds. Twenty. The music was making Marritt's headache worse. Leaning over, he shouted to make himself heard. "Excuse me! Could you turn that thing down?"

No answer.

"Excuse me! Could you turn it down a bit?"

The guy shouted back. "Hey, man, what's your problem? You don't like music or something?"

All Marritt wanted was to go home. It wasn't worth a hassle. Cursing silently, he got up and moved to a seat at the far end of the car. Jackson Heights. . . . Continental Avenue. . . . The subway rumbled on. At Kew Gardens, two black teenagers got on, smoking cigarettes. They weren't inhaling, Marritt noted. The sole reason they were smoking seemed to be so that they could stand directly in front of the No Smoking sign and blow smoke into the air.

Should I show them my badge? Forget it. I've got a headache. All I want is to go home.

"Hey, man!"

Marritt looked up and saw the macho white guy moving toward the black teenagers.

"Hey, man, that sign says no smoking. And your smoke's bothering my eyes."

Blaring music. Subway car wheels grating on tracks.

"Hey, white boy! What you gonna do 'bout it?"

Angry looks. Trouble. Marritt stood up. "Okay, fellows, that's all. I'm a cop." Reaching into his pocket, he drew out the gold shield that identified him as a detective and thrust it forward.

More angry looks, this time at him.

"Look, man," one of the teenagers shouted. "No one invited you into this."

"Hey, man! Just 'cuz we're black ain't no reason to beat on us. You're the po-lice, but that don't mean shit."

Warily, Marritt backed up a step and felt the weight of his .38-caliber Smith & Wesson revolver in its shoulder holster. A new alliance seemed to be forming, and he was the enemy.

Now the macho white guy was talking. "Hey, copper, I want you off this train!"

Marritt looked around. Except for present company, the subway car was deserted.

"Hey, man, you heard me. I want you off this train now!"

The subway was pulling into another station—Parsons Boulevard. "All I want is to go home," Marritt told himself. "I have no desire to make three arrests and spend the night at Central Booking."

The car doors opened. Slowly, Marritt backed toward the exit.

"All right," he muttered. "If you assholes want to kill each other, see if I care. Go ahead and do it!"

Chapter 1

New York: The last-gasp days of a brutal August. Muggy, oppressively humid. When Richard Marritt entered the 20th Precinct station house at 8:00 A.M., the temperature was seventy-five, soaring toward the high nineties.

His short-sleeved shirt clung to his chest. His entire body was drenched with sweat. Three times in the past week, Con Edison had ordered a citywide "brown-out," cutting electrical voltage by twenty percent. The combination of August heat and air-conditioning that was always too cold or not cold enough had given the detective a nagging cough.

The desk sergeant was his usual jovial self. ''The weather sucks,'' he announced as Marritt entered the station house.

Concurring wholeheartedly, the detective climbed the stairs to his second-floor office and began leafing through a stack of papers gathered on his desk. A particularly brutal rape. Two liquor store robberies. The telephone rang and Marritt picked up the receiver.

''Lincoln Center,'' the desk sergeant reported. ''It's a triple-header. Two men and a woman, dead.''

Ten minutes later, Marritt was at Lincoln Center for the Performing Arts. Moving past the New York State Theater and Avery Fisher Hall, he saw several squad cars and a fairly large crowd on the plaza ahead. Standard police procedure, he ruefully noted. Whenever a situation called for keeping people away, half a dozen cops could be counted on to drive their cars directly to the site and attract attention by flashing domed red lights. At the Metropolitan Opera House, he turned left and moved past the building to the edge of Damrosch Park. There, several wooden police barricades kept a group of onlookers at bay. Shouldering his way through the crowd, Marritt ducked under the first barricade and flashed his detective's badge to one of the cops.

''What happened?''

''Three dead,'' the cop answered. ''Two male, one female. One bullet each in the back of the head.''

''Who found them?''

"A maintenance worker."

Standing just inside the police line, Marritt surveyed the area. What passed for a park at Lincoln Center varied from the traditional format. Several rows of trees and shrubs were planted in sixteen-foot-square travertine encasements. Twelve of the encasements separated the Metropolitan Opera House from a cluster of black marble benches at the entrance to the park. Beyond that, the benches and trees gave way to a large outdoor stage with several thousand removable metal chairs facing forward. To the right, another travertine encasement thirty yards long separated the audience area from the side of the Met. The layout was such that a narrow isolated corridor stretched almost the full length of the opera house structure, cutting it off from the rest of the park.

"Down there," the cop said, gesturing toward the rear of the Metropolitan Opera House. "At the end of that corridor, you'll find three bodies."

Marritt turned and began walking toward another cop, who was standing at the fatal spot. Three figures lay crumpled at his feet. As Marritt approached, the cop stepped back, visibly grateful that responsibility for the carnage was about to shift to a senior officer.

"What's your name?"

"Haller, sir. Patrolman Michael Haller."

"I'm Richard Marritt."

"Yes, sir, I know. I've seen you around the station house."

Another sign of age. Young cops always knew the

names of older ones. And the older a cop got, the
less familiar he was with the names of junior officers.

"Did you check the bodies for identification?"

"No, sir. Sergeant Kroeber said we shouldn't touch
anything until you got here."

"I don't suppose you want to check them now
either?"

"If it's all the same to you, sir, I'd rather not."

Marritt bent over and examined the first corpse.
Male; late twenties; medium-length dark brown hair,
neatly cut. About five-foot-eleven, maybe an inch
taller. Blue jeans; a red-and-blue plaid shirt. A reddish discoloration, much like an ingrown scab, marked
the left underside of the victim's jaw. A handker-
chief, a comb; no keys, no wallet. Marritt turned the
body over. Freshly dried blood trailed from a wound
in the back of the head. Lead stippling (unburned
pieces of powder and lead) formed a circle three-
eighths of an inch in diameter. Shot from up close,
the detective noted—two feet, maybe a little closer.
Whoever did it wanted to eliminate any chance of
error.

Male victim number two. Same age as the other;
reddish brown hair; a beard, neatly trimmed. About
five-foot-nine, heavy. Brown pants, striped shirt.
Wound identical to that of victim number one. No
keys or wallet.

Last, the woman. Ten hours before, she must have
been a real looker. Long blonde hair; wide blue eyes;
tall, slender, good figure. Loose-fitting purple cotton
skirt, no pockets. A head wound like the males,

except without the stippling. Shot from about three feet away, Marritt estimated. Most likely, she was the final victim. The two men were shot first and the woman reacted, but not fast enough.

"Did you find a purse?"

"No, sir," Haller answered.

"Has anyone checked the area for wallets or identification?"

"Not yet."

A morgue ambulance drove onto the plaza and came to a halt. Two attendants exited from the vehicle and walked toward Marritt.

"Leave the bodies where they are," the detective ordered. Then he turned back to the younger cop.

"Haller, I want you to go out and coordinate a search of the area. See if you can find the keys and wallets."

"Yes, sir."

"And tell your fellow officers standing around by the barricade doing nothing that they should help."

Haller left. Ignoring the morgue attendants, Marritt began examining the foliage in the travertine encasement beside the bodies. Torn leaves; branches that were broken and compressed. Someone had made a home for himself in the bushes and, since the severed leaves were green with no trace of brown at the edges, the damage seemed to have been done the previous night. In all probability the bullets were fired from the shrubs after an accomplice had led the victims to the murder site.

"Okay," Marritt instructed the morgue attendants. "Do your stuff."

Body bags, white chalk marks—the ritual was familiar, always unpleasant. Another cop approached with a harried-looking middle-aged man dressed in civilian clothes.

"This is Wyatt Levine, director of security for Lincoln Center," the cop told Marritt.

The detective and Levine exchanged formalities.

"How many guards did you have on duty last night?"

"Ten men until midnight," Levine answered. "Five after that."

"Did any of them report hearing shots?"

"They all went home when their shifts ended. We won't know until they come back tonight."

Several more cops gravitated toward the shooting area.

"Someone said the blonde was good-looking," one of them reported. "Just wanted to check her out."

Twenty minutes passed. The morgue attendants went about their work. Marritt saw Haller coming back, his arm raised in a gesture of triumph.

"Found 'em," the young cop announced as he came closer. "Two wallets and a woman's purse—in a trash can over near Amsterdam Avenue."

"What about keys?"

"Nothing yet."

Slowly, Marritt thumbed through the first wallet. Driver's license: David Hollister; date of birth, January 21, 1956; address, 170 West 74th Street; height, six feet even; eyes brown/corrective lenses.

"Open up the body bag by the bushes," the detective ordered.

"Sir?"

"You heard me. Body number one—the one with the jeans and plaid shirt. I want to know if he has brown eyes and contact lenses."

One of the attendants did as instructed.

"He does," came the answer.

Marritt resumed looking through the wallet—a Chemical Bank Visa card, membership card for the New York Historical Society, miscellaneous papers, forty dollars in cash.

Wallet number two: Keith Swados; 10 West 95th Street. New York City Public Library card; expired driver's license issued by the state of Massachusetts, date of birth, March 2, 1954; a membership card for Local 802 of the American Federation of Musicians, seventeen dollars.

The purse: Rebecca Morris; 779 West End Avenue; age twenty-seven; Social Security number 067-38-8320. American Express card and MasterCard; an expired Juilliard School of Music ID card with her photo on it; another card, "In case of accident, please notify Mr. and Mrs. Jack Morris, 422 Kinney Lane, Calder, Ohio." Thirty-one dollars.

Marritt stared down at the body bags and wiped the sweat from his forehead.

"It wasn't robbery," he said at last.

One of the morgue attendants shrugged.

"It doesn't make sense," the detective muttered. "Why take wallets and then throw them away?"

"Maybe they didn't want us to identify the bodies." Marritt shook his head.

"Even without wallets, sooner or later we'd have made an identification. There has to be something more—like the keys; they're still missing. Maybe all someone wanted was to delay identification long enough to get a head start." The detective wearily pressed the tips of three fingers to his forehead. "I suppose it's time we looked at the victims' apartments. With the keys missing, I wouldn't be surprised if someone has beaten us to it."

Chapter 2

BEING A COP is like no other job in the world. It means being needed and scorned; risking your life in mid-afternoon, and going home for dinner with your wife and kids that night; serving as both target and the Great Protector. Do it right, and it's the most idealistic job imaginable. Marritt thought it was a wonder that all cops, himself included, didn't suffer from schizophrenia.

Most police work involves crimes that are anonymous—muggings, apartment break-ins. Even with most murders, next to no one cares. The victim's family suffers and the death upsets a couple of neighbors. But, generally, if someone is stabbed to death in Harlem, it's worth a paragraph at most in the daily press. Bring it downtown to a posh Fifth Avenue apartment, and on a slow news day it might rate a little more space; but even then the victim's name is soon forgotten. Crimes that capture the public imagination are few and far between. Marritt had the uncomfortable feeling that he was working on a blockbuster.

"Christ! Look at this! Front page of the *Daily News,* front page of the *Post;* even the *Times* put us on page one." Leaning forward, the detective surveyed the newspapers spread across his office desk. Twenty-four hours had passed since the three bodies had been discovered. Now, the morning after, the city was in a state of shock.

THREE MUSICIANS FOUND MURDERED AT LINCOLN CENTER, the *Times* read. TRIPLE MURDER AT THE OPERA, screamed the *Post*. Page 1 of the *News* recorded the first investigatory report: VICTIMS APARTMENTS WERE RANSACKED.

Looking up from the headlines, Marritt waited for a response from the tall, sandy-haired cop who sat opposite him.

Jim Dema was twenty years Marritt's junior, in his third year on the force. His father was dead; his mother lived in Brooklyn. The thing Marritt liked most about Dema was that he was a good cop. The thing Marritt liked least was that Dema was gay. "Be tolerant," he often told himself. "Don't think like some small-town Southern sheriff standing against the tide." Still, Dema's sexual orientation bugged him. "You have black cops; you have women cops; why should a gay cop be any different?" It was a question Marritt asked himself more than once, and the answer he always came up with was, "I don't know, but it *is* different." Be that as it may, Dema had been assigned to work with him on a regular basis, and Marritt was forced to admit they weren't a bad team.

Starting with the *Post,* the detective began reading aloud, jumping from point to point, looking up occasionally at his partner.

No known motive . . . A professional execution . . . Security guards at Lincoln Center report hearing nothing out of the ordinary the previous night.

Next, the *Daily News:*

Police confirmed that the victims' apartments were ransacked, apparently between the time of the shooting, estimated at midnight, and 7:00 A.M., when the bodies were discovered. . . . "It was a massacre," said New York City Chief of Detectives, Harvey Granfort. "A vicious crime in every sense."

Finally, the *New York Times:*

Three talented freelance musicians, all in their late twenties, were brutally murdered at Lincoln Center last night. The crime, which sent shockwaves through New

York's musical community, reminded many of the July 23, 1980, murder of violinist Helen Hagnes. But the Hagnes slaying was a random act by opera stage-hand Craig Crimmins, who sexually assaulted his victim before hurling her bound nude body down a Metropolitan Opera House ventilation shaft. By contrast, the latest slayings appear to have been a carefully plotted, calculated act.

Reading on, Marritt came to a thumbnail sketch of each victim:

David Hollister: 27; born in Milwaukee; trained at the Curtis Institute of Music in Philadelphia. Described by associates as one of the most promising young violinists in America. Member of The Devadutt String Quartet. Single; survived by his parents and two brothers.

Keith Swados: 29; born in Boston; trained at the New England Conservatory of Music. A cellist of virtuoso quality. Awarded the 1980 Greenburg Prize in international competition. *New York Times* music critic John Blessing once likened Swados' talent to that of a "young Pablo Casals." Single; survived by his mother, sister, and brother.

Rebecca Morris: 27; born in Calder, Ohio; trained at the Juilliard School of Music in New York. Initially a pianist, she began playing flute after a high school accident limited the dexterity of two fingers on her left hand. A member of The Nordlinger Quartet. Single; survived by her sister and parents.

"All right," said Marritt, putting the newspapers aside. "Let's take it from the top. Three freelance musicians are found dead at Lincoln Center. Each one was shot once at close range in the back of the head. Each was an exceptional talent and lived in New York. No one reports hearing shots, so we'll assume for the moment that the killer used a silencer. Silencers can only be put on automatic handguns, not revolvers, so there must have been spent cartridge shells at the murder site; but we couldn't find them. That means the killer picked up his brass. He was a professional. Add to that the fact that each victim's apartment was ransacked after the murder, presumably by the killer, and you get what?''

Dema shrugged.

"You're a big help," Marritt grumbled. "Let's see what else we've got. The bodies were discovered yesterday morning at six fifty-four A.M. Is that right?''

Dema looked down at the open manila folder on his lap and nodded.

"And what does the morgue estimate as time of death?''

"Midnight, give or take an hour.''

"Ballistics?''

"Their report isn't in yet.''

"What did we find in the victims' apartments?''

Again, Dema turned to the folder. "David Hollister —a large fourth-floor studio apartment; books, records, violin, stereo equipment, sheet music—''

"Okay, okay," Marritt said, cutting him off. "I was there. I take the question back. Let's look at it from another angle. What about motive? All three victims were musicians. Is it significant that the bodies were found at Lincoln Center? Are we looking for a psycho or a sophisticated criminal operative? Is it possible to reconstruct what the victims did the night they were murdered? How much did they have in common with one another?''

Dema sat silent as Marritt formulated his mental list.

"Who, if anyone, stands to benefit from their deaths? Did the blonde have any unusual sexual involvements? And just so you don't think I'm being prejudiced, check out the sexual involvements of the men, too. Except,'' Marritt added wearily, ''you can forget the sex angle, because these were cold, brutal murders without a trace of passion. And this case is going to be the worst ballbuster I've ever had. I can feel it.''

The telephone rang, and he picked it up. ''All right. . . . Yes, sir. Three o'clock. . . . I'll watch what I say.

"That was the Deputy Commissioner for Public Information,'' he advised Dema, when the receiver was back in place. ''They've scheduled a press conference for this afternoon at three o'clock.'' Shaking his head, the detective reached into the middle drawer of his desk for a seldom-used pad of lined yellow paper and began to write. ''I'm making a list,'' he announced. ''Things to Do— Number one, check with ballistics. Number two, identify close friends and associates of the deceased. Number three, reconstruct what each victim did on day of his or her death. Four, try to ascertain what, if anything, was taken from the victims' apartments. Five, check victims'

apartments and wallets for fingerprints. Six, interview next of kin.''

"I'm impressed," said Dema. "You're really
playing detective.''

Marritt raised his eyebrows just a bit. "I am a
detective," he grumbled.

Chapter 3

"LADIES AND GENTLEMEN. My name is Harvey Granfort, Chief of Detectives of the New York City Police Department. We've tried to accommodate as many of you as possible at this press conference. For those unable to attend because of limited space, it's being broadcast live on radio station WINS.

"As all of you know, yesterday morning at six fifty-four A.M., the bodies of three freelance musicians were found at Lincoln Center. Each victim had been shot once in the back of the head. Because of the high degree of public interest in the case, we've tried to accommodate the media by arranging this press conference. I'd now like to introduce Lieutenant Richard Marritt, the detective in charge of the investigation. Lieutenant—''

On cue, Marritt stepped to the podium and looked out at the sea of reporters, microphones, and television lights. He'd faced media audiences several times in his career, but they'd been nothing compared to this. The room was jammed; the atmosphere, electric.

"I don't have an opening statement," Marritt began. "Why don't you just ask questions, and I'll do my best to answer."

Then came the barrage.

"Sir, could you tell us what's been done so far to locate the murderer?"

"At the moment, we're gathering preliminary information from the ballistics laboratory, interviewing friends and neighbors, and the like. We're trying to learn what the victims did on the day of the murders and what, if anything, was taken from their apartments."

"Do you have any clues as to the killer's motive?"

"Not yet."

"Are there any suspects?"

"No."

"Was this the work of one individual?"

"At present, our guess is that more than one person was involved, but that's highly speculative."

"Would you say that the killings were planned, or the act of a deranged assassin?"

"Both. I don't think shooting three people in the head qualifies as a healthy psychological response."

No sooner were the words out of his mouth, than Marritt wished he could pull them back. The last thing he wanted was a wise-ass media image.

"Sir, are we correct in assuming that, so far, the police department has nothing concrete that might lead to solving these murders?"

"At present, the investigation is in an embryonic stage. We have nothing beyond that."

Marritt liked the word "embryonic." He wondered how long the press would let him get away with using it.

"Lieutenant, is it possible that the killer will strike again?"

That was a question he hadn't wanted.

"At this point," Marritt began slowly, "we have no way of knowing what led to the murders. There's no reason to believe that the killer will strike again, but I can't say that the possibility should be ruled out. What we're hoping is that anyone who saw or heard anything suspicious will come forward with the information. All leads will be kept in strictest confidence."

"Will your investigation be limited to persons associated with Lincoln Center and the New York musical community?"

"Definitely not. All members of the public had access to the murder site."

Judith didn't want to hear any more. Leaning forward, she flipped off the radio and stared at the headlines of the newspapers spread across her bed. There was no reason to believe that Klaus Ehrlich had anything to do with the murders. Most likely, he was some sort of front man for an eccentric patron of the arts or something like that. His offer had been completely harmless.

Still, she wondered.

Chapter 4

COPS SAY KILLER COULD STRIKE AGAIN. . . . COPS BAF-
FLED BY OPERA MURDERS. . . . POLICE ADMIT NO CLUES
IN LINCOLN CENTER SLAYINGS. . . .

Walking south along Third Avenue, Marritt reflected on the headlines that dominated New York
City's major dailies. The *Post*'s warning was unduly
alarmist. Yes, the killer could strike again, but it was
unlikely. Marritt had said as much at yesterday's
press conference. As for the *News* and *Times*, "baf-
fled" and "no clues" were accurate. Turning west

on 20th Street, the detective checked his watch and entered the eight-story New York City Police Academy. Enter To Learn. Go Forth To Serve read the motto in raised letters just inside the front door. Marritt flashed his detective's shield to the guard on duty and took the elevator to the top floor. There, a second guard examined the shield and pointed to the ballistics lab down the corridor.

After nineteen years on the force, Marritt was well-acquainted with homicide procedures. Whenever a firearms death occurred, the body was removed to the city morgue and x-rayed to determine the precise location of any bullets. In cases of multiple homicide, the same examiner performed the autopsy on each body. Then the bullets were marked with the first initial of the deceased's last name over the first initial of the examiner's, and forwarded to the ballistics laboratory.

At the end of the corridor, Marritt came to a small, square room with electric-blue walls. A tall dark-haired cop named Paul Miglione rose to greet him.

"Good to see you, Lieutenant. From what I hear, you've got a real ballbuster."

Marritt nodded and looked toward a set of optically paired microscopes mounted parallel to one another on a nearby desk. "Any luck?"

"The bullets just came in," Miglione answered. "I figured I'd wait for you before putting them under the microscope."

"I'm here."

Miglione reached for the first bullet—the slug that

had torn through David Hollister's brain—and slid it under the microscope.

"Thirty-two caliber," he said. "Let's see what the story is on class characteristics."

"Class characteristics," Marritt knew, referred to the number of lands and grooves, and a bullet's "twist." Each make of weapon had a particular number of lands and grooves, which rubbed against the bullet as it passed through the barrel, causing it to spiral like a well-thrown football.

Squinting into the eyepiece, Miglione adjusted several dials.

"It's an R-Four," he announced. "Four lands and four grooves twisting to the right."

Pondering the configuration, he scratched his head.

"That's an odd one. An R-Four that shoots thirty-two caliber bullets. There aren't many I can think of like that." As Marritt looked on, the technician reached for a thick loose-leaf manual on the shelf by his desk.

"Sauer & Sohn. . . . Bayard. . . ."

Laying the book aside, Miglione squinted into the eyepiece a second time, then turned to Marritt. "Given the diameter of the markings, I'd say what you have here is a thirty-two caliber Sauer & Sohn."

"What's that?"

"An automatic, German-manufactured—one of the few R-Four's around that shoots thirty-two caliber bullets. Six inches long, a little on the heavy side; ejects shells to the right, carries eight rounds. Deadly efficient."

"What about the other bullets?"

Miglione took the remaining slugs and put them
under the microscope, comparing them with the initial bullet.

"They're from the same gun," he said after a
moment's examination. "Bullet number three passed
through a lot of bone. There's a real deformity in it,
but the lands and grooves match up. Also, there's a
peculiarity on each bullet. Some sort of pimple inside
the gun barrel left its mark on all three slugs. Under
the microscope, it looks like a set of railroad tracks."

Moving back from the microscope, he gestured for
Marritt to take a look. The match was obvious.

"This guy was a professional," the technician
added. "One gun, three bullets, three victims instan-
taneously dead. Don't even bother looking for the
murder weapon. You'd never find it."

Back at the precinct house, Marritt compared notes
with Dema on the morning's events.

"I don't have much for you," the young cop said.
"The lab report on fingerprints is incomplete, but
looks negative. There's a memorial service at Saint
Paul's Chapel tomorrow, so we can interview next of
kin after that. I've been able to reconstruct what
Keith Swados did the day he was murdered, and it
isn't very exciting. Breakfast with a neighbor around
nine o'clock. Most of the day he practiced his cello.
Just after six, he went next door to borrow a stick of
butter."

"How come he didn't go to the store and buy it?"

Dema shrugged.

"What about after dinner?"

"No luck. And the neighbor swears there was no noise from whoever ransacked the apartment. Other than that, I set up an interview for two o'clock this afternoon with a woman named Jacqueline Whitlock. She's assistant manager of the New York Philharmonic. I figured maybe she could give us some help."

Reaching into his pocket, Marritt extracted the piece of paper headed "Things to Do."

"All right," he said, studying the list. "You follow up on the police lab. I'll start with Miss Whitlock."

Shortly before 2:00 P.M., the detective arrived at Lincoln Center. The police barricades had been removed a day earlier. Maintenance crews had washed away the blood. The only evidence of the three deaths was a bouquet of roses left by a mourner at the murder site.

Grumbling to himself about the heat, Marritt crossed the plaza to the back of Avery Fisher Hall, where he came to a set of steel doors marked Artists' Entrance. Inside, a security guard sitting beside a bank of TV monitors looked up. Marritt flashed his badge and received directions: "Go up the stairs to the next level; turn right. You'll come to an elevator that will take you to Miss Whitlock's office."

Following the course, Marritt rode the elevator to the sixth floor, and stepped out into a wide corridor with white walls and beige carpeting. Office cubicles and conference rooms flanked the corridor on either side. The detective saw a tall blonde woman walking toward him.

"Mr. Marritt, I'm Jacqueline Whitlock. Security notified me that you were on the way up. This way, please."

A bit uncomfortable with the unfamiliarity of his surroundings, Marritt followed her to a large office at the end of the corridor. There, Miss Whitlock pushed a button on a telephone by her desk and instructed a secretary to "hold all calls." She offered Marritt a seat, then positioned herself behind the desk and waited until he sat down. The room was spacious and well-decorated with all the trappings of authority and power. "The woman" (as Marritt thought of her) couldn't have been more than thirty, but she carried herself in a mature, distinctly aristocratic manner. Her hair was pulled back, and she wore a straight black skirt with a white blouse, white sandals, and black button earrings.

"Miss Whitlock," Marritt began. "As you're aware, three musicians have been murdered. Right now, we're gathering information. Let's take them one at a time. What can you tell me about David Hollister?"

Just for a moment, she seemed to grope.

"David—he was a wonderful musician. I had a lot of respect for him. He played violin with a quartet that was extremely well-regarded."

"Where did they play?"

"Most of their engagements were out of New York. In a typical year, they were on tour for four or five months. The rest of the time David substituted with various ballets and orchestras."

"Can you think of any reason why anyone might want to kill him?"

"Definitely not."

"What about Keith Swados? What was he like?"

"Keith was an incredible natural talent. He played cello for Orpheus—a New York chamber orchestra—and gave twenty or thirty solo performances annually."

"Can you think of any reason why anyone would want to kill him?"

"No."

"Rebecca Morris?"

"Rebecca was quiet; very talented. She overcame a tremendous physical handicap when she switched from piano to flute. Two years ago, she played on a summer tour with the New York Philharmonic. She was with us again for the parks concerts this past summer. Whenever one of our flutists was on vacation, we'd ask Rebecca to substitute."

"Did she or the other victims have any money problems that you're aware of?"

"All freelance musicians have money problems, Mr. Marritt."

"Outside of their professions, can you think of any common denominator that linked them together?"

Again, Miss Whitlock hesitated. "Not really; except that each of them was remarkably talented. Ninety-eight percent of the musicians in this city earn their living outside of the arts. David, Keith, and Rebecca were part of the other two percent. Do you understand what I'm talking about?''

Marritt shook his head.

"In the music business, Mr. Marritt, you have a small number of international stars—soloists like Itzhak Perlman and Pinchas Zukerman. They play when and where they want, and make hundreds of thousands of dollars. Below that, you have orchestra regulars—exceptionally gifted individuals who play full-time with the New York Philharmonic, Metropolitan Opera, and the like. David Hollister, Keith Swados, and Rebecca Morris fit into a third category—a middle group. They could have had jobs as regulars with any orchestra of their choosing, but that wasn't what they wanted. Instead, they performed with their own chamber ensembles and pursued the dream of becoming solo artists. That meant years of practicing and concerts at small colleges and YMCAs across the country. Once or twice a year, they might perform as soloists at Carnegie Hall or a comparable site. If Rebecca Morris made ten thousand dollars last year, she was lucky. Playing Bach cantatas at state universities isn't a big-money proposition. David and Keith probably did a little better, but not by much. What I'm trying to say, Mr. Marritt, is that these were rare individuals who sacrificed financial gain to expand their talents. Their deaths are a horror.''

Marritt waited, absorbing what was being said, until he was sure she had finished.

"How many musicians in New York City are in the same league as the ones who were murdered?"

"For each instrument, five, maybe six at most."

"And how many instruments are there?"

"Pardon?"

"You just told me, for each instrument, five or six musicians of their caliber. Now I'm asking, how many instruments are there?"

"You mean in an orchestra?"

"That's right."

"You want me to name them?"

"Please."

"Very well. There's violin, viola, cello, bass . . ."

Marritt reached into his pocket for a pad, and began taking notes.

". . . flute, oboe, clarinet, bassoon—"

"What's a bassoon?"

"It's a double-reed instrument, part of the woodwind family."

The detective had no idea what she was talking about. "Go ahead," he prompted.

"English horn, French horn, trumpet, trombone, and tuba."

"Drums?"

"Right—percussion and timpani."

"Is that all?"

"Plus piano and harp."

"So we're talking about sixteen instruments."

"That's correct."

Marritt did some quick mental arithmetic.

"And given five or six musicians of equal caliber per instrument, we're dealing with a pool of about ninety musicians. Could you get me a list of their names and telephone numbers?"

"I suppose so. In fact, I could give you our substitute list."

"What's that?"

"A list of freelancers approved by the music director of the New York Philharmonic. I can't promise that every name you want is on it, but it's fairly complete. David, Rebecca, and Keith were each listed."

"How soon can I have it?"

"Now, if you want."

"I'd appreciate that, Miss Whitlock. Otherwise, there's nothing more I can think of, unless you can think of something else."

They never thought of "something else." Marritt knew that from experience. Except—

"Mr. Marritt, there is one thing. I'm sure you've thought of this, but I read in the newspapers that the victims' apartments were ransacked. Did you find their instruments?"

"Yes."

"All of them?"

"I assume so. There was one violin, one flute, and one cello. And Rebecca Morris had a piano in her apartment."

"Mr. Marritt. David Hollister had *two* violins. One of them was quite valuable."

Marritt had the feeling that a new avenue of exploration was about to open up.

"How valuable?"

"It was a Stradivarius, worth three hundred thousand dollars."

Chapter 5

"HERE! I BROUGHT YOU A PRESENT."

Dema looked down at the two red tomatoes on Marritt's desk.

"My wife picked them from the garden last night. It's amazing what grows in Queens with water and a little sunlight."

Accepting the gift, Dema settled in a chair opposite his mentor. The memorial service for David Hollister, Keith Swados, and Rebecca Morris wasn't scheduled to begin until eleven, which meant he and

Marritt had two hours to talk strategy and compare notes.

"Our bedroom air-conditioner broke last night," Marritt announced, obviously intent on deferring police work. "Ninety degrees, muggy, and it goes on the fritz. I wanted to sleep in the kitchen with the refrigerator door open to cool off."

"What stopped you?"

"My wife. She's always nagging at me not to stand in front of the refrigerator with the door open. She gets it from her grandmother, who was born nagging. Ninety-one years old and she still nags; but what a worker! Even now she gets down on her knees to scrub the kitchen floor. And if you suggest using a mop, she tells you there's two things God wants you to do on your knees—pray and scrub the kitchen floor."

Dema waited, knowing that in due course Marritt would work his way around to weightier matters.

"Anyway, the air-conditioner's broken; my wife is making threatening noises about having the house painted; and I heard on the radio last night that the city is raising property taxes by one percent. Also, my wife and I turned our mattress this morning before I came in to work. That's something you're supposed to do every six months and, like clockwork, she remembers. That's what's happening at home. How about on the work front?"

"We've got a motive," Dema answered. "I checked out David Hollister's violins like you said. The one we found in the apartment was a backup, worth five or six thousand dollars. What we didn't find was the Stradivarius. It's worth a fortune."

"Says who?"

"One of his neighbors. Hollister bought it from a dealer named Maurice LePage, who owns a shop on Fifth Avenue. I've got an interview with him this afternoon at one-thirty."

"What else?"

"The members of Hollister's string quartet will be available at four o'clock."

"And?"

Dema looked down at his manila folder. "That's it. The only other thing I found out is that the discoloration on Hollister's chin was caused by rubbing it against his violin when he practiced. Apparently, if you play a violin eight hours a day, it hurts."

"All right," Marritt said, leaning back from his desk. "The memorial service starts at eleven. When it's over, you take next of kin; I'll interview this LePage character."

"What about Hollister's quartet?"

"Next of kin will take you most of the day," the detective answered. "I'll handle the quartet. And when you talk to the families, ask if they'll let us hold possessions from the apartments in a police warehouse until this thing is over. Not furniture, but books, personal papers—stuff like that. They might come in handy."

The memorial service at St. Paul's Chapel was investigatively worthless. Marritt arrived early and watched as the pews filled to overflowing. The mourners fit into three categories—the curious, those truly grieving, and the great majority who knew the victims casually and had come to pay their final respects. There were brief remarks by several speakers from New York's musical community, and a Schubert sonata tearfully played by one member each from the Devadutt and Nordlinger quartets. Afterward, Marritt made his way south to 51st Street, where the Maurice LePage showroom was located.

Old World was the image. Just past a small reception area on the top floor overlooking St. Patrick's Cathedral, a towering room beckoned. Large bay windows and a skylight flooded the area with light. A brass chandelier hung majestically from the ceiling. The walls were covered with walnut paneling interspersed with richly grained wooden racks holding violins, cellos, and other instruments. Oriental rugs covered most of the parquet floor. In the center of the room, an antique wooden table was draped by a well-worn maroon velvet cloth. Tactile by nature, Marritt reached out and touched a finger to the cloth.

"Mr. Marritt."

Caught in the act, the detective turned. An attractive man in his late fifties extended his hand.

"I'm Maurice LePage."

Marritt liked him instinctively. LePage was several inches shy of six feet, dressed in a brown suit perfectly creased. His hair was gray; his accent, French.

A gold watch; no wedding ring; loafers that looked like shoes Marritt had seen once in the window at Gucci's. Moving to an office off the main show-room, LePage bypassed an ornate, gold-leaf-trimmed desk and gestured toward two matching chairs. "A genuine tragedy," he said, as he and the detective sat. "What can I do to help?"

Marritt began slowly. "I'm at something of a loss," he admitted. "Three musicians have been murdered. I'm told that one of them—David Hollister—had a violin worth three hundred thousand dollars, and that he bought it from you. That violin is missing now, and I'd like to know what you can tell me about the market for stolen instruments. I'd also like to know why anyone would pay three hundred thousand dollars for a piece of wood, and where David Hollister got that much money."

In the room next door, a cello was being played.

"Perfectly valid questions," LePage answered. "Let me deal with the easiest first. David Hollister was a brilliant violinist. As such, he had many admirers within the musical community. It's not unusual for corporate donors and private foundations to make generous contributions toward the purchase of a string instrument. Generally, the gift is conditioned on the recipient repaying his benefactors if his income rises above a certain level. In David's case, Exxon and the DuMare Foundation made generous grants. If my recollection is correct, the purchase price of his instrument was two hundred ninety thousand dollars, and it has appreciated considerably in value since then.''

"What would a thief do to sell it?"

"That, Mr. Marritt, depends on the thief. Most stolen instruments are sold to pawnshops for fifty or a hundred dollars. Generally, the pawnbroker recognizes the instrument for what it is and calls the police. Other times, when a thief learns how valuable the instrument is, he's shocked into returning it.''

"Somehow I don't think this particular thief will shock that easily.''

"Then the instrument will, as you Americans say, go underground. No reputable dealer will touch it, nor can it be played in public. A stolen Stradivarius is as easily recognized as a stolen Rembrandt. Each one has characteristics as unique and varied as a statue by Michelangelo.''

"Why are they worth three hundred thousand dollars?"

LePage held out his hands, palms up. "Why is a painting worth five million? Any reasonably competent craftsman can make a violin. And any reasonably competent painter can create a Rembrandt—if he happens to be Rembrandt. Antonio Stradivari learned his craft in Cremona, Italy, as an apprentice to the great Nicolo Amati. He died in 1737 at the age of ninety-three, after producing one thousand instruments, seven hundred of which remain today. We know precisely how Stradivari made his violins, with one exception—we cannot duplicate the varnish, which is crucial to the tone of the instrument. Also, and this may sound strange to you, a good string instrument requires a period of at least forty years for the tone to be played in. A truly superior violin requires two hundred. In London, there is a Stradivarius worth one million dollars. In my own inventory, I have twelve, ranging in value from two hundred thousand to eight hundred thousand dollars.''

"You *own* them?"

"Seven are mine. One is to be sold for a Swiss client. The other four are here for restoration. You must understand, Mr. Marritt, Stradivari is my passion. All my life, I have tracked his creations. Some are in museums; others are with orchestras or in private hands. I have read every guide, followed every lead. As far as is humanly possible, I know the location of every Stradivarius on this planet.''

"All except one," Marritt answered.

Out on the street, Marritt checked his watch (three o'clock), and bought two hot dogs from a vendor for lunch. Then, gathering his thoughts, he walked up Fifth Avenue. By prearrangement, the surviving members of the Devadutt Quartet were waiting in a practice room at the Juilliard School of Music. Paul Bradford, Katherine Billings, Ira Reynolds—viola, cello, and second violin, respectively. They were still in shock, still unbelieving. "It could have been any one of us," Ira said.

There were no trick questions. Marritt spoke directly and accepted each answer at face value.

"We formed the quartet three years ago," Bradford told him. "David and I had been together in another ensemble that fell apart, so we tried again with Katherine and Ira. We didn't have a leader. No one tried to impose his will on the others. The Devadutt Quartet was a cooperative venture.''

"It's totally illogical,'' Katherine Billings offered. "Why David? Why Keith and Rebecca?''

"How well did you know the other victims?''

"Keith and I auditioned together several times,'' Katherine answered. "He was better than I was. Rebecca kept pretty much to herself, but the few times we met she seemed wonderful.''

"Did any of you speak to David on the day he was murdered?''

They hadn't.

"Do you have any idea why he might have been at Lincoln Center that night?''

Same response.

"What about arguments, fights, anything like that? Did David Hollister have any enemies?''

"David was the sweetest guy in the world,'' Ira Reynolds told Marritt. "The whole time the quartet was together, there was never a dispute. The only thing he ever did that struck us as wrong happened about a month ago. *He wouldn't say why, but for some reason David canceled out on a concert we'd planned for early November—the week of November fourth.*''

"Was there any significance to that date?''

"Not that I know of.''

Judith stood in front of the mirror, and checked the angle of her arm to make certain her bow passed exactly parallel to the bridge of the viola. More often than not, she practiced while standing. It increased her concentration. A pile of yesterday's clothes lay on the floor. The telephone rang and she ignored it. She knew the music well now, enough so that she didn't need pages except for an occasional reference. She had succeeded in shaping the piece into a whole, and was able to play it through over and over until it flowed. The third movement was the most difficult: turbulent, bold. Her fingers and bow moved so quickly that they were almost impossible to follow visually. But her notes were clear, each one sounding for the briefest moment before it was gone. Two hours passed. Judith lay her viola down. She rested for ten minutes, ate a blueberry muffin, and then practiced for two more hours, stopping occasionally to make a penciled notation on the manuscript; making everything whole. *"When I play, I am the music."* Instrument in hand, she could recreate sounds that sprang from the genius of Mozart and Bach centuries ago. With more primitive instruments, she was capable of reaching back to ancient Egypt and transporting herself to the banks of the River Nile.

The piece was extraordinary. She loved it. Still, there were times she was frightened.

She wished she hadn't taken the ten thousand dollars from Klaus Ehrlich.

Chapter 6

H E LOVED THEM—but God, the kids could be difficult.

Jonathan was behaving pretty well at the moment, but eight-year-old David was on a roll. Marritt wasn't quite sure how to handle him.

"David, eat your eggs. A good breakfast makes you healthy."

"I'm already healthy."

"Eat them anyway. And drink your milk."

"Why?"

"Because I said so."

"That's not a good reason."

"All right. Drink your milk because I said so, and because there are people dying of thirst in the Sahara. Drink your milk because I love you and want you to grow up to be big and strong. Also, drink your milk because it will give you energy to clean up your room, which better be done by the time I get home tonight or else you're in big trouble."

Rebellion.

"It's *my* room. Why do I have to clean it up?"

"How many reasons do you want?"

"Seven."

"Okay. Number one, clean up your room because I said to. Number two, clean up your room because it's a mess. Number three, clean up your room because you have certain assigned chores in this house, and cleaning up your room is one of them. Number four, clean up your room because your mother is tired of doing it for you. Number five, clean up your room. . . ."

Marritt left the house just after seven, and walked to the subway station. The heat was breaking; the late August humidity was gone. Waiting for his train, he bought a copy of the *Daily News*. For the fourth day in a row, a story connected with the Lincoln Center murders had made the front page: $300G VIOLIN STOLEN! screamed the headline.

Just before 8:00 A.M., Marritt arrived at the precinct house and climbed the stairs to his office, where Dema sat waiting. Preparatory to their conversation, the detective spooned some instant coffee into a Styrofoam cup and filled it with hot water. "No sugar," he announced. "I'm on a diet." Then, settling behind his desk, he waited for Dema to pull his chair closer.

"I saw next of kin yesterday," the junior cop reported.

"And?"

"Nothing. I tried for five hours. What you have are parents who loved their children but weren't involved in their day-to-day lives. They're as confused and stunned as everyone else. Ditto for the sisters and brothers."

"Did you ask permission for us to hold onto personal belongings?"

"Yes, sir, it's no problem."

"Anything else?"

"I went through the substitute list you got from Jacqueline Whitlock at the New York Philharmonic. All totaled, it has ninety musicians. Add thirty or so friends and neighbors, and it should take us about three weeks to interview everybody. I've set up six interviews for this afternoon. Also, this might not sound like much but, for what it's worth, it seems as though less than half of the classical musicians in this city live alone. Most are married, have live-in lovers, or share an apartment to help meet expenses. David Hollister, Keith Swados, and Rebecca Morris all lived alone. That might be coincidence; it might be something more."

Marritt weighed the item before pushing it to a corner of his mind from where it could be recalled on short notice. Then he focused on the day at hand. "All right. I'll handle the interviews set up for this afternoon. Why don't you get a list of rare-instrument dealers nationwide, and give each of them a call. Maybe we'll get lucky on David Hollister's violin. Otherwise, just keep doing what you've been doing— it's fine."

The interviews were dead ends—all of them.

Iris Tidmore, cellist, thirty years old: "Keith Swados and I played chamber music together a few times," she told Marritt. "He was very happy with his cello, a brilliant performer. That's all I know about him."

George Tanney, French horn player: "David Hollister was like most good musicians. Music dominated his life. As for Rebecca, I met her once at a restaurant called Summer Rose. She was gorgeous."

Andrew Kosmovsky, violinist, age thirty-four: "I know what I read in the newspapers; nothing more."

Claire Bluest, harpist, age twenty-nine: "A lot of people knew Rebecca. When someone is that talented and that good-looking, she attracts attention. But really, she was very shy; she kept to herself mostly. I'd be surprised if anyone knew her well."

Lawrence Sapery, another violinist: "I knew Keith Swados fairly well. He told me once that he was afraid of losing his individuality if he spent too much time playing in orchestras, sitting with eight other cellists in a row. But the last time I saw Keith was months ago."

Gordon Engel, bassoonist: "I played with each of them at one time or another. Can I think of anything that might help? Not at all."

At day's end, Marritt returned to the station house, rearranged some papers on his desk, and prepared to go home. Dead bodies, musicians, three hundred thousand dollar violins. David Hollister had been murdered for his instrument; that much seemed pretty certain. But it didn't explain why Keith Swados and Rebecca Morris had died with him. A loose end was gnawing away at the detective's insides. Picking up the telephone, he dialed Directory Assistance and asked for the Manhattan phone number of Jacqueline Whitlock. Moments later the operator responded. "I'm sorry. There's no listing for a Jacqueline Whitlock in Manhattan."

"What about the New York Philharmonic Orchestra?"

Several minutes and two switchboard operators later, Jacqueline Whitlock was on the line.

"I'm sorry to bother you," Marritt began, "but I need some information. What was the dollar value of Keith Swados' cello?"

There was a long pause.

"That's hard to say. If I remember correctly, it was an eighteenth-century Guadagnini, worth somewhere in the neighborhood of a hundred and fifty to two hundred thousand dollars."

"And what about Rebecca Morris' flute?"

"I don't know what kind she had."

"What's the maximum it could have cost?"

"Flutes are relatively inexpensive. Certainly, no more than ten thousand dollars."

Putting down the receiver, Marritt played with the puzzle at hand. Three musicians with no significant ties to one another had been murdered. The stolen violin explained Hollister's killing. But why wasn't Swados' cello gone? Maybe it was too big to carry. On the other hand, Rebecca Morris' flute was small. Maybe they'd left that because of its value—"only" ten thousand dollars. But if all they'd wanted was a violin, why was it necessary to kill at all?

Labor Day Weekend passed; the interviews continued.

Gayle Kiley, trombonist: "David and I were classmates at the Curtis Institute in Philadelphia. Even then, he was a polished musician, and that was eight years ago, when he was nineteen."

Edwin Farrar, oboist, age twenty-nine: "Keith and I had dinner together a few weeks before he died. Nothing seemed wrong."

Christine Rosen, violinist: "I've talked about it a lot with friends. I mean, when three people are killed and you know them, it's real and unreal at the same time. But no one I've talked with has any idea what happened or why."

A check of pawnshops was a waste of time. Dema reported on his survey of rare-instrument dealers nationwide. "Zero," he told Marritt. "All of them know about the murder. If the violin's for sale, it's out of the country or underground."

David Hollister's last day was reconstructed. Breakfast, practice from ten in the morning till two in the afternoon, a movie, dinner with a friend. "Chinese food," the friend remembered. "Afterward, we took a walk. Around nine, David said he had a few things to do and went home."

"What sort of things?"

"He didn't say. Just things."

More interviews. Dema's manila folder began to bulge, leading Marritt to suggest they invest sixty-nine cents in an expansion file to keep papers from spilling onto the floor. The *New York Post* ran an "exclusive" on "The Investigation to Date." Three pages were devoted to reporting that the police were no closer to solving the murders than they had been on the day the bodies were found. "The investigation," a police source was quoted as saying, "is going slowly but surely—and you can forget the surely."

Dema agreed to forego the vacation he'd been planning until the investigation was further along.

More interviews.

Howard Maxwell, Vice President of Archive Records: "We're a small company devoted to chamber music," he told Marritt. "David Hollister and his quartet recorded two albums for us. Both were well done. Neither sold particularly well."

Jerome Millikan, sixty years old: "Rebecca Morris studied with me at Juilliard. She was marvelously gifted, an ideal student. To take up the flute in late adolescence and do as well as Rebecca—one can only wonder what might have been had she begun earlier, or lived on.''

Elizabeth Casanoff, musical agent, interviewed at her office on West 57th Street near Carnegie Hall: "Keith Swados was one of my clients. As an agent, my job is to book concerts and arrange tours. On average, Keith gave twenty to thirty solo concerts a year.''

"Can you think of any reason why someone might want to kill him?''

"Not at all. Keith wasn't the sort of person who made enemies.''

"Was there anything unusual going on?''

"Not really.''

Marritt paused. "What do you mean 'not really'?''

"Nothing. It's just— Well, this is a bit embarrassing, but I did have the suspicion that Keith might have been planning to change agents. In the music business, it happens all the time. Money is scarce; performers don't get what they deserve. Sometimes a musician feels that a different agent will do a better job. Keith never said as much to me directly, but I had the distinct feeling he was testing the waters, letting another agent arrange a concert or two without my knowing.''

"What makes you say that?''

"Feminine intuition,'' Casanoff answered. "Plus one thing more. There was a week this coming autumn, right in the middle of the booking season, that Keith asked me to keep open. I asked why and he gave me—maybe I'm just imagining this—but it seemed he gave me a slightly guilty look. Then he said something about a personal matter."

"Do you remember when that period was?"

"Not offhand. But I could check my records."

"Please."

Marritt waited.

Elizabeth Casanoff opened up a large loose-leaf notebook and began turning pages. "Here it is. *Keith told me he'd be unavailable from November fourth through November ninth.*"

A trombonist—nothing.

Another violinist—no help at all.

Marritt looked at his note pad, where he had written down the dates he had gotten from Keith Swados' agent. "November 4 through November 9." Vaguely, they stuck in his mind. He wasn't sure if he'd heard them before or had simply imagined their sound. So many interviews, so many names. It was humanly impossible to remember them all.

Four o'clock. One more interview, and then it would be time to go home. He was up to interview number forty-nine, at 306 West 87th Street—a violist named Judith Darr.

The building was a four-story brownstone. Marritt opened the front door and stepped inside. A buzzer system linked to each apartment was attached to the vestibule wall. The intercom was marked by a sign that read, "temporarily out of order." Marritt pushed the button next to "J. Darr—4C," and waited until the buzzer sounded, then climbed the stairs to the top floor. In the doorway to 4C, a young woman stood waiting. Marritt flashed his badge and introduced himself. The one saving grace to these interviews was that they'd been well-coordinated. Dema had seen to it that, when Marritt arrived, someone was always waiting.

Inside the apartment, the detective looked around. It was an airy studio, with windows open on the far wall. A sofa bed, bookshelf, two hundred or so record albums. A brown-and-gold area rug covered the hardwood floor. Scattered across the dresser top were jewelry boxes and small bottles of cologne.

"Would you like some coffee?"

Marritt shook his head and settled in a chair by the door. Vertical slats dug into his back, and he shifted position to make himself more comfortable. The woman was young, in her mid-twenties. About five foot five, wearing jeans and a Mostly Mozart T-shirt. Her face was plain, but he liked it: brown eyes, a narrow nose with a slight bump on the bridge, a small mouth, teeth that were flawless. She moved like a dancer, with graceful, measured steps. Her long brown hair was pulled back and piled atop her head in a manner that suggested she didn't care how it looked.

"Miss Darr, as you know, we're investigating a triple murder. Each of the victims was on the substitute list for the New York Philharmonic. You're on that list as well. I'm not sure where that gets us, but I'd like to ask you a few questions."

"Go ahead."

"All right. First, I'd be interested in knowing what you can tell me about each of the victims. Did you know David Hollister?"

He'd asked and heard answers to the same questions dozens of times before. By now, he could conduct the interview in his sleep. Judith Darr impressed him as articulate and bright, like most of the women he'd met on the case so far. A bit nervous, but that was understandable in light of the subject matter. Like the others, however, she had nothing to offer. She wanted to help; he sensed that. She was trying to give him something, but the words didn't come.

"Can you think of any reason why this might have happened?"

"No."

"Did any of the victims have any enemies that you're aware of?"

"No, sir."

"Were they involved in any sort of sexual scandal?"

"Not that I know of."

The wooden slats were starting to hurt his back.

"Did you ever hear about anyone making threats against any of them?"

"No."

"Were any of them involved in prior incidents of violence?"

"No."

"Did they have any involvement with gambling or drugs?"

"Not that I know of."

His questions were reaching beyond all logical expectations and Marritt knew it. It was time to go home.

"All right, Miss Darr. I have no more questions. If you think of anything, feel free to contact me at the Twentieth Precinct."

The detective rose wearily from his chair. Judith walked him to the door. He wasn't even sure it was worth asking, but what the hell—

"One more question, Miss Darr. Do the days November fourth through November ninth mean anything to you?"

From the look in her eyes, Marritt knew he had struck gold.

Chapter 7

THEY SAT ON THE SOFA in Judith's apartment, facing each other. "All right," Marritt said softly. "I want you to start from the moment you entered the restaurant, and tell me everything that happened."

"What do you want to know?"

"I just told you. I want it all."

Judith tugged at the belt on her jeans. "It was in late June. I told you that a moment ago. I got there, and Klaus Ehrlich was alone at a table in the corner, with his back to the wall so he could look out over the entire restaurant.''

"Go on."

"We ordered from the menu. He had some kind of veal; I had salmon. That's silly to remember, but I don't go out to good restaurants very often. After we ordered, he asked a few questions about my background. He probably knew more about me than he let on. At least, I had that feeling. Then we started to talk about music. Afterward, he made me the offer."

"Had you seen him before—at a concert, on the street, outside your apartment?"

"No."

"How did he act when he was with you?"

"Very gracious, but stiff, proper."

"And his clothes?"

"A gray suit—conservative, not stylish."

"People don't go around offering strangers ten thousand dollars for legitimate business purposes. You know that, don't you?"

"I thought—I— He could have been some sort of Michael J. Anthony type, who went around giving away millions of dollars. That's how I rationalized it."

She was starting to weaken, trembling beneath the surface. Marritt sensed it and let up a little. "What happened the second time he made contact?"

"The following morning he called like he said he would. I told him I'd decided to accept his offer, and he asked where it would be convenient for us to meet. I said my apartment."

Marritt's face showed disbelief. "You let him into your apartment!"

"I let you in, didn't I?"

"I'm a cop!"

"It was a risk. I knew that. The whole thing was a risk. But I don't have rich parents to bail me out. What was I supposed to do—meet him at a nice safe place like Lincoln Center by Damrosch Park?"

"Okay," Marritt told her, backing off. "What happened when he got to the apartment. Where did he sit?"

"By the door. The same chair you took."

"And what happened?"

"It was very quick. He said he was delighted I'd agreed to join in the project. He asked if I owned a black evening gown, and I said yes. After that, he told me to make sure the evening gown was ready in November, and also that I'd need a valid passport. Then he gave me the money."

"In what form?"

"Cash—hundred-dollar bills."

"What did you do with it?"

"I put it in the bank."

"And the music?"

"After I took the money, Ehrlich handed me the score. He warned me again not to tell anybody. Then he left."

"Did you tell anyone?"

"No."

"How did you feel when you took the money?"

"Excited, scared. It was ten thousand dollars. I'd never seen that much money before."

"Did it occur to you to ask if he could be contacted?"

"I did; the answer was no. He said I'd be contacted just prior to November fourth."

Marritt took a deep breath, then let it out. "You're in pretty deep water, you know that?"

Judith nodded.

"Do you have the music?"

"Yes."

"I'd like to see it."

Judith stood up and crossed to the dresser. Inside the top drawer, about fifty neatly drawn sheets of music were bound together.

"Here," she said, coming back.

"Is this the only copy?"

"Yes."

Marritt took the score and thumbed through it. The musical symbols could have been Chinese characters for all they meant to him. "What kind of music is this?"

"I'm not sure. As best I can tell, it's a symphony with everything but the viola part whited out."

"Who wrote it?"

"I don't know. It's very moving, very powerful. The first thing I did after Ehrlich left was play the music. It has some incredibly difficult rhythmic configurations and complex passage work, but I don't recognize the composer. Maybe if I had the whole symphony, the other instruments, I'd know."

Marritt leafed through the music a second time. There was no publisher's imprint on it. Of all the loose-screw cases he'd ever worked on, he told himself, this one headed the list. Except it wasn't simply a loose-screw matter. More and more, it seemed to be a carefully planned, calculated plot. And it scared him.

Judith was talking: "When I heard about the murders, I think I knew. But I hadn't been hurt, and I talked myself into thinking there wasn't any connection. And now—" Her voice filled with quiet desperation. "What should I do?"

Just for a moment, something in Marritt made him want to reach out and hold her, to tell her that, scared and vulnerable as she was, he'd protect her. Don't worry, he wanted to promise. But he couldn't, not in good faith, because something frightening was happening and he was beginning to feel that the other side might be more powerful than he was.

"Help me, please!"

"Miss Darr, I'll do what I can. Right now, I'm as lost as you are. All I can say is, if someone wanted to kill you, they'd have done it twelve days ago. You're safe—for now."

Chapter 8

AT NINE O'CLOCK the following morning, Marritt helped Judith into the blue-and-white squad car outside her apartment and slid into the backseat beside her. "This is Jim Dema," he announced, nodding toward the driver. "We're on the case together."

When the door was shut, Dema pulled away from the curb and began driving downtown toward police headquarters. Judith sat silent, looking out the window at the tall buildings on either side. You've really done it, she told herself. You've gotten yourself in a lot of trouble.

Marritt and Dema were talking about the weather, then sports, finally the murders. "We're going to see a police artist," the detective told Judith. "With a little luck, he'll be able to construct a fairly accurate portrait of your friend Klaus Ehrlich."

Dema drove south, then east across Chambers Street until they reached the Municipal Building. "See you this afternoon," Marritt told the younger cop. Then he and Judith got out of the car, and walked through the Municipal Building arch to One Police Plaza. In the lobby the detective flashed his shield to a uniformed cop and led Judith to a bank of elevators. On the fifth floor, they got off and walked down a corridor. The building, with its cinderblock walls, resembled a fortress. They came to a door marked Artists' M.O. Unit, and Marritt ushered Judith inside, through a large room with thirty or so desks, to a small office. Three drafting tables stood against the far wall. At the first one, a young man wearing blue slacks and a black V-neck sweater sat waiting.

"This is Patrolman Yannas," Marritt told Judith. "He's one of three police artists for the City of New York."

The drafting tables were cluttered with objects— black plastic ashtrays, sketchbooks, pencils of varying sizes. Yannas offered Judith a seat, and Marritt stepped aside.

"Miss Darr," the artist began, "everything I put

on paper this morning will have to come from your head. How long were you with the suspect?''

"About two hours," Judith answered.

"Under what circumstances?"

"In a restaurant, then later at my apartment."

"So for most of the time, you were at eye level."

"That's right."

"Was the suspect wearing a hat?"

"No."

"Glasses?"

"Yes."

"How old was he?"

"About forty; maybe a little older."

"Did he look like someone you know, or someone whose picture we can use as a reference point?"

"No."

Yannas reached for a pencil and began to sketch the rough oval shape of a head. When the simple outline, without features, was complete, he added a loop on either side. "Are the ears in the right place?"

"I think so."

"All right. We're about to draw in three stages. The first stage will put features in their proper place, nothing more. Then we'll try to make the nose look like the suspect's nose, the mouth look like his mouth, and so on. Finally, with shading and detail work, we'll bring the portrait to life. What was the suspect's hair like?"

"Fairly short; brown and gray—parted on the left."

"Did it cover his ears?"

"No."

"How was it combed?"

"To the sides."

Yannas began building the top of the head. "Did his hair fall or was it neatly combed?"

"The latter."

"Like this?" he asked, filling in the outline a bit.

"Put the part a little more to the left."

The artist did as ordered. "All right. Now let's drop down to the mouth. Give me a start."

"He had thin lips," Judith offered, "and a small mouth."

"Was the top lip bigger or smaller than the lower?"

"They were equal."

"Did the line of his mouth curve up or down?"

"It was even." She watched as he sketched. "That's not what it looked like. I was wrong. The bottom lip was thinner."

Yannas made the correction. "Now tell me about his eyes. What color were they?"

"Hazel, I think."

"What else do you remember about them?"

"They were round."

"Everyone's eyes are round," the artist prompted.

"The sockets, the lids—they were rounder than most."

Yannas talked as he sketched. "The width of the average human face is five eye-lengths. And the edges of the mouth come to the center of the irises. A person can grow a beard or cut his hair, but without plastic surgery he can't change the basic proportions of his face." After the eyes, he sketched in the rough outline of a nose. "All right, Miss Darr. What we have here is a face. Not his face—a face. Let's pretend it's a piece of clay and work with it." The artist reached for a formbook by the side of the table and opened it. "This page has twenty-nine sets of eyes. Which ones look most right?"

Judith studied the photos. "The sockets were like number seven," she answered. "The eyebrows—that's hard. Their shape was like number four, but they were close to the eyes like twenty-eight."

On Yannas' sketch paper, Klaus Ehrlich's right eye became the first well-developed feature.

"And the pupils were larger," Judith said. "Almost dilated, like he'd been to an eye doctor for drops."

The artist continued to sketch. "I'm making the eyelid droop a bit. Is that right?"

"I guess so. It's hard to tell because he wore glasses."

"We'll come to that later. In the meantime, stop me if the drawing starts to look less like the suspect at any point." One eye was already finished. Yannas penciled in the other, giving them both a slightly melancholy look. "Very often," he explained, "eyeglasses cover up the eyebrows and make them seem thinner than they really are. Is this right?"

"Yes."

"Good. Now the nose." He turned the formbook to another feature sheet. "Here are forty noses. Which one is best?"

"Number thirty-six."

Yannas drew a horizontal line midway between the eyes and mouth. "This line indicates where the nose ends. Is it positioned right?"

"Yes."

The nose took shape. Straight bridge, small rounded nostrils. Then the mouth.

"He had a dimple on his chin," Judith added suddenly.

"What about the overall shape of his head? Is it right?"

"Not quite. It was rounder than you have it. And he was older."

"We'll get to age later. Right now, I want to stay with shape."

"His head was rounder," she repeated. "I'm sure of it. He was thin, but the line from his jaw to his ear was fuller than this."

"What about the hairline?"

"It was lower than the way you have it. And the hair was shorter."

With a kneaded eraser that looked like putty, Yannas ran his hand across the sketch. Ehrlich's jawline became fuller, and the length of his hair diminished.

"Now the glasses. Were they ordinary or bifocal?"

"Ordinary."

"What kind of frames?"

"Rimless, I think. No, wait! They weren't rimless. They had gold frames, thin and rounded."

Yannas took a sheet of tracing paper and placed it over the sketch, utilizing a technique that would enable him to take the glasses on and off until they were just right. Judith watched.

"A little smaller," she said. Then, "That's perfect."

He copied the glasses onto the original sketch.

"What do you think?"

Judith stared at the drawing. "It's— I don't know. The face is too young. Something's not right."

"Okay. Let's bring him to life."

Blending, shading, rotating pencils of varying widths, Yannas began filling out the sketch. Crow's-feet around the eyes, lines between the nose and mouth, wrinkles on the forehead, eyes more deeply set—all signs of an average forty-year-old man. Judith watched transfixed.

"Is there anything else you'd like added?"

"Around the eyes—a few more lines. And near the nose, some blood vessels were cracked— You've got it! That's Klaus Ehrlich!"

Three hours had elapsed. Yannas printed his name in the lower right-hand corner of the sketch and beneath that, added:

> Sketch No. 1795
> Police Report No. 138009
> Witness—Darr, Judith
> Lieutenant Richard Marritt

Then he sprayed the sheet with a Krylon additive to keep it from smudging and handed the paper to Marritt.

"Thanks," said the detective.

"Don't thank me. Thank the witness. She was terrific."

An auxiliary cop drove Judith home and dropped Marritt at the 20th Precinct station house. After a quick lunch, the detective returned some telephone calls and conferred with Dema.

"We're on our way," the young cop reported. "This morning I ran a computer check on all New York City banks. David Hollister had an account with Chemical. On June twenty-fifth, he deposited ten thousand dollars. Four days later, Rebecca Morris put ten thousand dollars in a Chase Manhattan Money Market account."

"What about Keith Swados?"

"Nothing yet, but I'll bet my salary we find it. Meanwhile, I found out what Rebecca Morris did the day she was murdered. It's what you'd expect, except for one item. That night she had dinner with a friend, who says she seemed exceptionally preoccupied. The friend asked what the matter was, and Rebecca told her she was worried about a business venture."

"A business venture?"

"Right—which made no sense at all, since Rebecca was hardly a venture capitalist. Then she told the friend that what she meant was that a very profitable performance might be about to fall through, and she didn't want to talk about it."

Marritt let the thought sit. "All right. I guess we

concentrate on Klaus Ehrlich. Run his name through every computer available, and see how many people with the same name turn up. Then ask the phone company to put a computer tap on Judith Darr's wire. If he calls again, I want a trace on the number.''

"What about the composite sketch? Do we make it public?''

Again, Marritt was silent. ''That's a tough one,'' he said at last. ''Right now, Judith Darr is our only link to three murders. If Ehrlich calls, I want her to follow through on his instructions, which means I don't want him scared off. For the time being, let's keep his face out of the newspapers. Circulate the photo through the FBI and Interpol, but not to the media. After that, we'll see what happens.'' Weighing his options, the detective looked at his watch, pondering what to do next. It was four o'clock. ''How'd you like some overtime?'' he asked his partner.

"What sort?''

"My guess is whoever ransacked those apartments was looking for Klaus Ehrlich's music. Now that we know a little more about the case, let's check the police warehouse and see if there's anything they forgot to take.''

An hour later, the two cops were in the Bronx. The warehouse was dusty and dimly lit. Marritt figured that more than one rat's nest was within reach, but he didn't want to know about it.

"Over there," said Dema, "those cartons in the corner. There's one for each apartment."

Together they struggled to bring the first carton to the middle of the room. "Dump everything on the floor," Marritt ordered. "Then we'll put it back, piece-by-piece." Straining, they turned the carton over and watched David Hollister's belongings spill forth. Books, records, letters, sheet music. "Let's start with the music," Marritt prompted. "Maybe there's something that matches Ehrlich's."

Bach. Brahms. Mozart. Wagner. One-by-one, they went through the sheets. Beethoven. Schubert. Haydn. Lizst. Each piece bore a printer's imprint. On every one, the composer was noted. Then came the books, followed by Hollister's personal letters. There was correspondence from an old girlfriend in Milwaukee, and letters from another in Detroit. For two hours they reconstructed David Hollister's life. Then, straining again, they moved the carton back and started on Keith Swados' belongings.

"Think positive," Marritt exhorted. "Something will come up." But he didn't believe it, not really, because police work consisted of making your own luck, and he didn't feel particularly lucky at the moment. "There has to be something," he told Dema. "Let's look at it from all angles; let your mind wander."

"Toward what?"

"Anything. Put yourself in Klaus Ehrlich's place. I did that once. I'd just made detective and was trying to track down a child-molesting murderer. Two kids dead, not a clue in sight. Christmas was coming and I asked myself, 'What job would I want if I was a child molester?' Then I figured it had to be a department store Santa Claus, with kids coming up all day and sitting on my lap. We checked it out and, sure enough, we got him, dressed up as Santa. So put yourself in Ehrlich's shoes. What was he looking for? What might be incriminating in this pile of junk?''

''There's a problem,'' Dema cautioned.

''Which is what?''

''Klaus Ehrlich ties in with this, but someone else could be the killer, someone dedicated to stopping whatever it is Ehrlich is trying to accomplish. Maybe that's the reason Ehrlich considered secrecy so important to the project. He could have been as frightened as anyone else.''

''From what you've heard,'' Marritt grumbled, ''does Klaus Ehrlich sound frightened?''

Carton number two was returned to the corner at ten o'clock. Nothing of investigative value had been noted. ''One more to go,'' Marritt prodded. ''In three months, it'll be Christmas. The overtime will do you good.''

Rebecca Morris' belongings were next. Music. More music. Records. Books. If anything in her possession had matched Klaus Ehrlich's score, whoever ransacked the apartment had found it.

''What are you looking at?''

Marritt looked up as Dema's voice interrupted his thoughts. ''A picture,'' he answered.

Actually, there were several photos. Rebecca with a friend, hiking in the woods. Rebecca alone, standing on the beach. A close-up of Rebecca smiling. She'd really been quite beautiful, Marritt thought. And now two cops were going through her belongings like scavengers in a garbage dump. Near the bottom of the pile he came to her datebook. In January, she'd been dating some guy named Sam—at least, it looked that way because Sam appeared every Saturday night for four or five weeks. Then Sam disappeared, and most Saturdays were empty, except for two dates with David and one with Roger. Weekdays were spent practicing, with a fair number of evening rehearsals and concerts. And then Marritt realized that, despite anything else, there were times when he was very stupid. Because here he was, checking out Rebecca Morris' social life, and maybe what he should do instead was turn the datebook to November.

The hour was midnight.

A thin blue ink line spanned the days November 4 through November 9. And beneath the line was one word followed by a question mark:

BEETHOVEN?

Chapter 9

THE MID-MORNING SUN sent sharp rays of light scurrying across the apartment floor. Judith stood in front of the mirror. She'd been trying to practice for two hours, but the music wouldn't flow. Klaus Ehrlich kept intruding on her thoughts.

Greed and need. Those were the reasons she'd taken the money. That, plus the seduction of performing in Europe. Now all she wanted was to be left alone. The intercom buzzed. Nervously, she hit the button to identify the caller.

"Richard Marritt," the voice sounded. "I'd like to speak with you, Miss Darr."

Three flights of stairs later, he was at her door. She'd never given much thought to cops before, but now she was glad to see one. Beneath Marritt's gruff exterior, she sensed a soft inner core. And Marritt had a gun. He could protect her.

"I'm sorry to bother you," the detective began, "but several things have developed since the last time we talked. It now looks as though each of the victims received ten thousand dollars, although in the case of Keith Swados we're not sure. We don't know if the killers were working with Ehrlich or trying to thwart him, but my guess is that Ehrlich had the same business arrangement with each of the victims that he has with you, and that they violated one or more of the conditions. Probably, they learned the music, and even if they hadn't, there was still time to meet the November due date. Condition two was that they be available to travel to a European city between November fourth and November ninth, which they were planning to do. That leaves condition number three—that they tell absolutely no one about the project. I wouldn't be surprised if somehow the victims communicated with one another. If that happened, and Ehrlich found out about it—" Marritt's voice trailed off. "Miss Darr, I'd be less than honest if I didn't tell you what you already know—your life is in danger."

"What—what do I do?"

The detective shrugged, not from a lack of concern, but because he genuinely didn't know. "That's up to you. Right now you're our only hope for solving these murders. If Ehrlich learns you're cooperating with the police, he could be very hard on you. There's no way I can guarantee your safety, but if you play this thing out, maybe we'll get to the bottom of it. More than anything, it will take a great deal of faith on your part."

"You're asking a lot."

"I won't argue with that. But, realistically, if somehow you managed to drop out of the project, they could still kill you."

They stood facing each other.

"All right," Judith answered. "What do you want me to do?"

For the next few hours, they talked. "I need your help," Marritt told her. "I want you to tell me everything that could have gone on in those musicians' lives. On an average day, what did they do?"

"They practiced music."

"For how long?"

"Six hours a day. You have to understand, playing an instrument is ninety percent drill and muscle coordination. David, Rebecca, Keith, all of us—we practice finger movement the way ballet dancers work on their bodies. The worst thing in the world that could happen to us would be to hear something in our heads and not be able to execute it."

"Do you get bored?"

"Hardly ever. While the rest of the world is at

work soldering rivets and waiting on tables, we're sitting at home playing music. At rehearsals we're surrounded by people caught up in the same beautiful flow. I don't think you understand the gratification inherent in harmony and sound."

The detective pressed on. "When you practice alone, do you hear the way the other instruments should be playing?"

"Sure."

"What about the music Ehrlich gave you? Can you imagine that as part of a whole?"

Just for a moment, her eyes seemed to cloud over. "I've tried. I can't tell you how often I've tried to imagine the total sound. It's wonderful, that much I know. But I don't know what the other instruments are doing. That's one reason I'm agreeing with you to go on with the project."

"Could Ehrlich's music be Beethoven?"

"No."

The rapidity of her response caught Marritt by surprise. "How can you be so sure?"

"Because I know Beethoven. I've studied his music all my life. He's the greatest composer the world has known."

"You're not answering my question. How can you be sure it's not Beethoven?"

"Because everything he ever wrote is catalogued and written down. No other musician's life was as well documented from early adulthood on."

"Suppose I told you that Rebecca Morris put a

note on her calendar suggesting that the music was
Beethoven?''

"Then I'd tell you Rebecca was wrong. The music
is good. In places, it even sounds like Beethoven.
But I've studied every piece Beethoven wrote, and
this isn't one of them.''

"You're sure?''

"Positive.''

Back at the station house, Marritt straightened the
clutter in his police locker, then listened to Dema
report on his own morning and what he had found.

"First off,'' the young cop began, "I've checked
with some people on Judith Darr. She's highly re-
garded within the profession—very accomplished for
someone twenty-six years old. Word is, she stands a
good chance of winning a Pro Musicis Scholarship,
which carries a fairly substantial financial award. As
for Klaus Ehrlich, the name is too common to give us
a hand. The phone books in Europe are full of them—
seventeen Klaus Ehrlichs in Frankfurt alone.''

Running a hand across the back of his neck, Marritt
waited as Dema went on.

"I've also looked into Keith Swados' finances a
second time. There's still no sign of ten thousand
dollars. I suppose it's possible that the money was in
his apartment, and the killers took it when they ransacked the place; but that's a guess, nothing more.''

"Is that everything?''

"Yes, sir; except—well, one thing bothers me

about what we've found. So far we've identified four
people who met Klaus Ehrlich, and all four accepted
his offer. There has to be someone who turned him
down. But who—and why haven't we heard about it
by now?''

Marritt sat silent for a moment. Then he consulted
his notebook, slowly picked up the telephone, and
dialed the number of the New York Philharmonic.

Dema waited.

"Jacqueline Whitlock, please. . . . Hello, Miss
Whitlock. This is Richard Marritt of the New York
City Police Department. I wonder if you could tell
me something. Have there been any deaths from
illness or accident in the past few months that you
know of? I'm interested in musicians about thirty
years old. . . . That's right. . . . What can you tell
me about him? . . . Thank you.''

Very deliberately, Marritt lay down the phone.
"Once upon a time," he began, looking toward Dema,
"there was a cellist named Arnold Buxton. He died
in a freak elevator accident—this past June.''

Dema said nothing.

There was a glimmer of fear in Marritt's eyes.
"Look, Jim. I don't know if Buxton's death was
planned or accidental, but we seem to have fallen
into pretty deep water. For the time being, let's be
careful the undertow doesn't drag us down.''

Chapter 10

"WE'RE HAVING THE PAINTERS," Marritt grumbled. "Nine years, we've been in the same house without having it painted. I wanted to make it ten, but my wife said do it now. What a mess! The whole house stinks. There're drop-cloths on every floor. You can't find anything, because everything's stuck under piles of furniture."

The desk sergeant listened sympathetically as Marritt rambled on.

"For two days, it's been a zoo. And the painter is

some old guy with arthritis, so it'll be that way for two days more. Yesterday and the day before were my days off. I wanted to work in the garden and watch the kids play ball. Instead, I cleaned closets and scrubbed floors. That's a part of the deal I'll never understand. You clean up before the painter comes, and then he makes such a mess, you have to clean up all over again after he's gone.''

His story told, Marritt went upstairs to wait for Dema, who arrived at nine.

"How were your days off?" the young cop asked.

Whereupon Marritt told his tale of woe a second time.

"It sounds wonderful," Dema prodded. "I'm sure the kids were extremely helpful."

"Right! David in particular liked the fact that he couldn't watch television because the set was upside down under a ladder that was wedged in between the sofa and a wall.''

"You're exaggerating."

"That's what you think! Painting is worse than nuclear war. The only good thing about it is that it took my mind off Klaus Ehrlich. But now that I'm back, what's going on?"

"The pieces of the puzzle are being found."

"Wonderful! Now stop being cryptic and tell me what happened.''

Reaching for the brown expansion file that had succeeded his manila folder, Dema turned to page one. "I checked out Arnold Buxton. He was a cellist, thirty-one years old; lived alone on the West

Side. On the night of June twenty-first, he was killed in an elevator accident at his apartment house. No one saw it. The police report was based on a reconstruction, with the help of the building manager and an electrical engineer. Apparently, what happened was that Buxton took the elevator to his apartment on the fifth floor. When the car door opened, the elevator was several feet below corridor level, so Buxton decided to climb out rather than ring the emergency bell. The elevator dropped, crushing his body between the car door and air-shaft wall.''

"Were there signs of sabotage?"

"Not that anyone found. And nothing indicates that Buxton received ten thousand dollars. Either it was an accident, or Buxton said no to Klaus Ehrlich."

"And was replaced by Keith Swados."

"Right—which brings us to Mr. Swados. We already know that cellos can cost up to half a million dollars. Do you have any idea what people pay for a bow?"

"What's a bow?"

"That stick they use to vibrate the strings and make the cello sound. A cheap one costs fifty dollars. A diamond-studded one once sold for a hundred thousand. The average for top-flight string-instrument bows is between five and fifteen thousand dollars. In early July, according to Maurice LePage, Keith Swados bought a bow for ten thousand dollars—cash."

Marritt's eyes widened.

"Before you get angry," Dema cautioned, "LePage was pretty decent about the whole thing. He called from his showroom yesterday afternoon. The transaction was off the books to save sales tax; that's eight and a quarter percent in New York. Besides, where the murders were concerned, LePage had no idea that money was involved. After he saw you, his conscience bothered him. He thought the information might be relevant, so he called. That's all.''

For a good ten seconds, Marritt sat silent; then he reached for the phone.

''Who are you calling?''

''Judith Darr.''

''What for?''

''Among other things, to tell her I'm going to return Klaus Ehrlich's music. She'll have to practice if she's going to perform.''

It was a ten-minute walk from the precinct house to Judith's apartment. ''Is it all right if I eat while we talk?'' Judith asked when the detective arrived. ''I've got a rehearsal just after noon.''

''Be my guest.''

As Marritt looked on, she opened the refrigerator and took out a container of boysenberry yogurt. ''I used to be a vegetarian,'' she said, spooning the yogurt into a bowl. ''But not anymore.'' A small basket of fruit lay on the kitchen counter. Judith took a banana, peeled it, and sliced the fruit into the bowl. Next a peach, slightly rotting on one side. ''What the hell, either I eat it now or never.'' The sliced peach joined the banana and yogurt. ''Do you want some?''

"No, thanks," Marritt told her. "I'll get a slice of pizza later on."

They sat at a formica-topped table, Judith with her back to the refrigerator, Marritt with his to the wall.

"Miss Darr," the detective began, "we now know that, like the other victims, Keith Swados received ten thousand dollars. In other words, within the space of ten days, Klaus Ehrlich doled out forty thousand dollars in cash. That's a lot of money, and I wouldn't be surprised if—well, let's leave it at that for now. I've brought you back Ehrlich's music. Jim Dema and I made one copy. The original is yours."

"What am I supposed to do with it?"

"That's up to you."

"Did the other victims have the same score?"

"We don't know."

To Marritt's surprise, Judith smiled. "It's funny, I was thinking about the music again last night. That's all I seem to think about lately—the music and Ehrlich. Keith Swados played the cello and David was a violinist. With my viola and Rebecca's flute, you'd have a flute quartet."

The detective's eyes widened.

"But don't get excited," Judith added. "Ehrlich's score has dozens of places marked *divisi*. That means whoever wrote it contemplated a second viola. It's not a quartet." Lifting a spoonful of yogurt to her mouth, she glanced at Marritt. "Are you sure you don't want any?"

"No thanks. I grew up in a generation when yogurt was a funny word."

"All right, if you won't eat, there must be something I can do for you. Maybe you'd like to come to my rehearsal this afternoon?"

"What for?"

"If you're serious about learning what it's like to be a musician, this is your chance. I'm a substitute violist for a small orchestra. They do a dozen concerts each year. Besides," she added, "since the murders, I've been imagining weird people following me around. There's nothing I'd like more than a police escort for a few hours."

The rehearsal auditorium was warm and well lit. When Marritt and Judith arrived, sixty or so musicians were already on stage tuning their instruments in a cacophony of sound. Marritt settled in a seat midway back on the center aisle and looked around. The performers were young, dressed in skirts and jeans, everyday garb. Half of them were recognizable from interviews he'd done.

"Places!"

On command, the multitude of instruments fell silent. Then, with the conductor giving instructions in a vocabulary Marritt didn't understand, the music began. Mozart? Brahms? The detective wished he knew what they were playing. He didn't like not knowing what was going on.

Klaus Ehrlich. Three bodies. Flute quartets. What if Ehrlich were putting together a full orchestra? How many musicians would that involve? A hundred maybe—times how many thousands of dollars? Their instruments alone could be worth ten million dollars, maybe more.

The music was building. Marritt focused on Judith Darr. She was lost in the sound—happy, joyous, at peace with her world. He was too far away to see her clearly. What he saw was the contour of her cheeks and maybe the direction of her eyes, not much more.

"Sir."

Marritt turned. A young woman stood over him.

"Sir, Patrolman Dema wants to see you at the station house right away. He says it's important."

Two hours later, Marritt was waiting outside Judith's apartment when she returned home. "I have to show you something," he told her. "And be very careful before you make up your mind."

"I don't understand."

"You will in a moment."

Wordlessly, he reached into an envelope and pulled out an eight-by-ten-inch glossy photo.

"That's him," Judith whispered. "That's Klaus Ehrlich."

"Are you sure?"

"Positive."

Marritt's face looked weary and worn. "His name's not Ehrlich; it's Karl Heiden. Two years ago, a plane owned by an Austrian nobleman named Victor Pesage crashed in the Atlantic Ocean. Heiden was the only reported passenger. Searchers found debris from the plane and the body of the pilot, but Heiden's body was never found. Pesage was a well-known patron of the arts, and in later years something of a recluse.''

''And Heiden?''

''Prior to disappearing, he was Curator of the Beethoven Museum in Bonn.''

Chapter 11

THERE WAS A LOT ABOUT MARRITT that Dema liked. Not that the detective was a progressive thinker—he wasn't. But his straight-ahead style had a certain charm, and Dema appreciated the fact that most days at the precinct house began with a personal touch.

"My wife spilled a glass of wine in bed last night," the detective announced. "Every now and then, she gets sophisticated and drinks wine with her crackers instead of milk."

"Red or white?"

"White, thank you—which doesn't mean it wasn't a mess. Changing sheets was easy, but the mattress got soaked. We had to hook up the hair dryer to dry it out."

Dema waited, as he always did, for the conversation to turn to police work.

"Did you see the newspaper this morning?" Marritt demanded.

"Not yet."

"Well, in case you're wondering, the National Rifle Association is at it again. What a bunch of assholes! Now they're against outlawing devastator bullets. I know a guy who heads up one of the local NRA chapters. Back in Korea he got drunk and drove a jeep off a cliff, so they gave him a Purple Heart. Now he spends all his time preserving the right to bear arms, while cops get shot with devastator bullets." The telephone rang, and Marritt picked up the receiver. "How should I know?" Dema heard him grumble. "Maybe they got it from someone at Lincoln Center. . . . That's right; the official line is there's no known link. . . . The reason that's the official line is because it's true. Anything else is sheer speculation. You can quote me on it.

"That was the Deputy Commissioner for Public Information," the detective said when the receiver was back in place. "Someone leaked the Arnold Buxton story to the *New York Post*." Reflecting for a moment on the potential for panic inherent in the situation, he shrugged. "Anyway, I suppose it's time we got to work. What's new on our friends Victor Pesage and Klaus Karl Heiden Ehrlich?''

"Right now," Dema answered, "it's still fragmentary. Heiden is German—a musical scholar and archivist with a top-flight reputation. Seven years ago, at age thirty-five, he was named Curator of the Beethoven Museum in Bonn. The appointment caused quite a stir, partly because of his age and partly because Heiden wasn't the friendliest fellow around. Two years ago, he was reported killed in a plane crash in the Atlantic Ocean. That's where Pesage comes in.''

"How so?''

"Pesage is an odd one. He was born in Austria; he's loaded with dough. His parents trained him to be a violinist, but World War Two interrupted his studies. Then, in 1947, he enrolled at the Mozarteum in Salzburg. That's a well-known music academy.''

"Go on.''

"Pesage's experience at the Mozarteum wasn't good. Apparently he didn't play very well. After a faculty committee recommended that he withdraw from school, he spent a number of years as a society figure and patron of the arts in Vienna. Over time, he became something of a recluse, and his behavior grew more erratic. He also developed something of an interest in reincarnation. As best anyone knows, he's still alive, never married, fifty-six years old.''

"How does Pesage tie in with Heiden?''

"Apparently, three or four years ago, Pesage began some sort of research project that brought him to

Bonn. He and Heiden spent a considerable amount of time together, and Heiden took several trips in Pesage's private plane. It was on one of those trips, with Heiden the only passenger reported on board, that the plane went down.''

"Where does Pesage live now?"

"No one's sure. He owns several mansions and guards his privacy extremely well. Most of what's known about him relates to his days in Vienna. The rest is guesswork and speculation.''

For a good ten seconds, Marritt sat silent. "I should have been a fireman,'' he finally muttered.

"Yeah, but think of all the fun you'd have missed. . . . Hey, where are you going?''

Without explanation, the detective was up from his chair and headed toward the door. "For another conversation with the only lead we've got in this case— Judith Darr.''

More often than not, police work is uneconomical. Unproductive leads take days to track down. Cops spend hours sitting in court waiting for petty cases to be called. Walking to Judith's apartment, it occurred to Marritt that he should have telephoned to see if she were home. But he wanted to walk; fresh air was always welcome.

When the detective arrived, Judith was in, wearing jeans and the same Mostly Mozart T-shirt he'd seen her in before. This time, though, he noticed her figure. Maybe her image was more in focus now that he was starting to know her better.

"Miss Darr, I know we've discussed this before, but the past few days have raised the question again. How can you be sure the music you've been given isn't Beethoven?"

The certainty of her response was unchanged. "Because I know Beethoven. I've studied his work my entire life. I know every piece Beethoven wrote, and this isn't one of them."

"Isn't it possible he wrote something you don't know about?"

"Not at all."

The look of frustration was evident in his eyes.

"Look," Judith said, softening her tone. "I suppose it's possible that someday someone will find something Beethoven wrote when he was twelve. But the music that came from Ehrlich is developed and mature. It couldn't possibly be Beethoven."

"Why not?"

"Because Beethoven's music is known. From age thirty on, he enjoyed unparalleled fame as a composer. His letters were preserved; his every move was scrutinized. For the last eight years of his life, even his conversations were written down."

"His conversations?"

"That's right. Don't you understand? *Beethoven was deaf!* The illness began when he was a young man and grew worse and worse until, at the end, he couldn't hear at all."

Marritt's eyes widened.

"Don't you understand?" Judith repeated. "You're talking about the most brilliant composer the world has ever known. His Ninth Symphony is the greatest orchestral triumph of all time; but Beethoven was stone deaf when he wrote it. During his last years, everything people said to him had to be written down. Otherwise, he wouldn't have known what they were saying. Hundreds of notebooks have been left behind in volume form. And through them and everything else recorded about his life, everything Beethoven wrote has been found and accounted for."

They stood silent, facing each other.

"All right. You're the expert, Miss Darr."

"I'm sorry. I want to help, really I do. But there's no point in rewriting history to lead you on."

A few minutes later, Marritt was gone. After he'd left, Judith went to the kitchen, sliced an orange into sections, and ate them one by one. It was time to practice. She wanted to play something different from the norm. Something special, something turbulent and bold. Ehrlich's music was in the dresser drawer. She knew it by heart; there was no need for the score.

Anticipating the flow, Judith cradled her viola in her arms. She wished she had other parts besides just the viola. Why couldn't Ehrlich, or Heiden, or whatever his name was, have given her more? Maybe Beethoven had written the music at night when everyone thought he was asleep. That was a marvelously romantic notion. But if the music was Beethoven, why hadn't he told anyone he was writing it?

It wasn't Beethoven. She knew that.

But she wasn't quite sure.

He wasn't anything if he wasn't stubborn. Tenacity was one of the traits on which Richard Marritt prided himself.

Down Broadway, over to Amsterdam Avenue. Just south of 65th Street, he came to the Lincoln Center Library. Through the revolving door; into the lobby. A huge sign hung on the wall above:

> 1st Floor Reading room; circulating library; reference
> assistance.
> 2nd Floor Reading and listening area; children's library.
> 3rd Floor Research library.

Inasmuch as he was there for research, it made sense to start on the third floor. Elevator to three. Marritt got off. A huge glass partition separated a reading room from the corridor. Eight long tables were evenly spaced on the floor. Down the corridor; into the room. The card catalogue was marked "Special Collection." Taking a seat at the first table, Marritt looked around. Several readers were engrossed in silent study. Total silence. An anorexic-looking woman with long hair approached and pointed to the sign by Marritt's arm: "This table reserved for staff use only."

"You can sit at the table over there if you'd like."

Marritt stood up self-consciously. Maybe he'd take a look at some of the books on the shelves. None of the titles seemed relevant. Leaving the glass-partitioned room behind, he made his way further down the corridor. He could always flash his badge to one of the librarians. "Excuse me: I'm Richard Marritt of the New York City Police Department. I wonder if you could tell me a little about Beethoven." It would never do.

The next reading room had more glass partitions. Marritt wondered if this was how a mouse felt when it was trapped in a maze. Maybe another floor would be more hospitable.

The first floor proved less intimidating than the third. At least it looked like the libraries Marritt had known. There were rows of shelves and no glass partitions. On the north wall, Marritt saw the master card catalogue, and approached it to look up "Beethoven." Slowly, he thumbed through the cards:

Beethoven's Letters; from the Collection of Ludwig Nohl.
Beethoven's Briefe: In Auswahl Hrsq. Von Leitzmann.
Beethoven: Samtlicha Briefe; kritische Ausgabe mit Erlauterungen.

He needed help. Reluctantly, Marritt moved toward the reference librarian. "Excuse me. Could you tell me where to find books on Beethoven?"

"Which aspect of his music are you interested in?"

"Everything."

"Two aisles down, sir, on the right."

Two aisles down; turn right. There were six shelves that held hundreds of books—all about Beethoven. Book number one: *Die Klavier—Sonaten Beethoven*. Then another: *Beethoven und die Unsterbliche Geliebte*. Fewer than half were written in English. Marritt took one of the less threatening titles down from the shelf. The musical vocabulary was completely beyond him. "Polyphony," "counterpoint"—words he didn't understand.

"With God as my witness, if anyone finds out what I'm about to do and makes fun of me, I'll kill him."

Marritt rode the elevator to the children's library on the second floor. Low metal shelves; he had to bend over to reach them. Midway down the third aisle, he came to the section on Beethoven. There were seven books—each one in English—and they were understandable.

Beethoven: Great Musician—"for children age 5 through 7." He'd skip that one.

The Life of Ludwig van Beethoven—a biography, 180 pages long. That was better.

Beethoven's Symphonies—maybe.

He wouldn't be doing this, Marritt told himself, except that three people had been murdered. Pursuing the investigation was his responsibility, and something Dema had told him stuck in his craw: "Over time," Dema had said, "Victor Pesage became something of a recluse. The few people who saw him reported that his behavior was quite erratic. He'd also developed an interest in reincarnation.''

Marritt was afraid he might be dealing with a homicidal maniac who thought he was Beethoven.

Chapter 12

SPREADING THE *New York Post* ACROSS HIS DESK, Marritt read the lead article aloud to Dema:

MET MURDERS—COPS PROBE GRISLY CORPSE

Sources close to the investigation of three murders at Lincoln Center revealed today that police were examining a fourth death for possible ties to the bizarre slayings. On June 21, Arnold Buxton, a thirty-one-year-old cellist, died in what was believed to be an elevator accident

at his West 62nd Street apartment. However, recent
events have led police to suspect foul play in connection
with Buxton's death. Lieutenant Richard Marritt, the
detective in charge of the investigation, has denied the
reports. "There's no known link between Buxton's death
and the murders; anything more is sheer speculation,"
Marritt said yesterday. However, other sources took
issue with the detective's remarks.

The article continued for several paragraphs, closing
with:

Chief of Detectives Harvey Granfort said that he was
satisfied with the progress of the investigation. "For the
time being," Granfort told reporters, "the case will
remain under the command of Detective Marritt."

"For the time being!" Marritt muttered. "Shit! If
those other sources want this case, they can have it."

"They're jealous because they can't get their names
in the newspapers," Dema said with a grin.

Marritt started to answer, then simply gave his
partner a dirty look.

"I did some follow-up work on Victor Pesage,"
Dema said, seeking to change the subject. "He last
appeared publicly at a charity ball two years ago in
Vienna."

"And?"

"And what?"

"And what else did you find?"

"There isn't much. In fact, outside of what I told
you the other day, it's negligible. The only new
information ties in with Pesage's interest in reincar-

nation. Four or five years ago, he began contributing heavily to a European foundation for psychical research. Around the same time, he told several associates that he had a strong personal interest in the subject. What Pesage meant by that wasn't clear, but he left the impression that he was intrigued by the possibility of prior lives.''

"In other words, he's a nut."

"Not necessarily. We've called in psychics ourselves to locate bodies in missing persons cases. There's a woman in New Jersey who does it for state troopers all the time. Sometimes she misses; sometimes she hits.''

"And you believe in that crap?''

Dema shrugged. "There's a foundation in New York that devotes all its resources to psychical research; and the government has made several studies.''

Marritt sat silent, weighing options. "All right,'' he said at last. "Since there's a homicidal maniac running loose, why don't you set up an appointment for me with a psychic nut expert. Make it for this afternoon, at four o'clock, if possible.''

The morning passed. Dema made several telephone calls, then went out to pursue his own interview list. Marritt drank two cups of coffee, then reached into his desk for *The Life of Ludwig van Beethoven*. Like most biographies written for children, it began with a detailed description of its subject's childhood. Beethoven was born in December 1770, the second of seven children, four of whom died in infancy. His father was a musician, who gave lessons to Bonn's aristocratic youth. His grandfather had directed a local orchestra. Beethoven spoke German and was "of Flemish extraction." His father sought to develop him as a performer, and at age six the boy gave his first public concert on the clavier. ("What's a clavier?" Marritt wondered.) In his teens, Beethoven held a series of court-appointed musical apprenticeships and studied both violin and clavier. ("That word again.") He was also employed by a widow named Helen von Breuning as a music instructor for her four children. The job gave him an entrée to society and an introduction to Count Ferdinand Waldstein—a confidant of Maximilian Franz, whose brother was Joseph II, the Holy Roman Emperor. ("I hope I don't have to remember all these names," Marritt murmured.) In 1792, Maximilian Franz sent Beethoven to Vienna—"the capital of music." For two years, he studied under Joseph Haydn and accumulated patrons in high places. Finally, in 1794, at the age of twenty-four, he composed three trios he thought worthy enough to combine and title "Opus I." "These first simple piano trios," the biography noted, "were followed by 137 more numbered works."

Setting the book aside, Marritt checked his watch. It was twelve o'clock; the entire morning had been wasted. Maybe some lunch would do him good.

The early afternoon was spent on interviews.

Meredith Hartsburg, bassoonist, age thirty: "I never met Rebecca or Keith. David Hollister was friends with my roommate. You interviewed her right after the shootings three weeks ago.''

Allen Zuckerman, violinist, twenty-nine: "Keith Swados and I used to play Scrabble together. Neither of us was very good. I have no idea why anyone would want to kill him. Do the days November four through November nine mean anything special? Not that I know of.''

A flutist—nothing.

A harpist—no help.

At four o'clock, Marritt arrived at the American Society for Psychical Research on 73rd Street just off Central Park West. The building was an elegant, five-story townhouse with wrought-iron-framed doors.

"Dr. Racah is expecting you," the receptionist told Marritt. "Upstairs on the second floor—the room to the right.''

Following instructions, the detective made his way up the circular staircase to a large room on the second floor. Two bay windows, partially obscured by drapes, overlooked the street. Otherwise, except for the fireplace and door, the walls were completely lined with books. A brass chandelier with painted bulbs hung from above. The center of the room was dominated by a heavy antique wooden table, with six straight-backed chairs set around it.

"It's good to meet you, Lieutenant. What can I do for you?''

Dr. Joshua Racah was approaching age fifty. He had gray hair, a full beard, and wore a tweed jacket with matching slacks.

"I'd like this kept in strictest confidence," Marritt began, sitting at the table opposite Racah. "I'm here because there's an outside chance that this city has a lunatic who thinks he's Beethoven."

Racah's gaze didn't waver. "That's not as uncommon a fixation as you might think."

"Maybe not. But this particular lunatic is shooting people in the head. I'd like to know what we might expect from someone who believes in reincarnation."

Again, the gaze—straight ahead. "Mr. Marritt, from a scientific point of view, reincarnation is wholly undocumented. Very few parapsychologists believe in it. I myself do not."

"So where does that leave us with someone who does?"

"If what you're looking for is the influence of a deceased personality upon the living, I suggest you consider the phenomenon of possession." Warming to his subject, Racah leaned forward. "Possession, Mr. Marritt, is best explained in three stages. Someone dreams a very vivid dream about a friend's death, and then learns that it occurred exactly the way he dreamt it. Or an entire family is looking for a piece of jewelry that a dead relative has left behind. All of a sudden, someone gets a flash that the jewelry is hidden in a hollowed-out book on the living room shelf—and sure enough, it's there. These are examples of *sensitivity* to the dead. A more advanced stage is known as *haunting*. Voices are heard; objects move. Someone imagines a little old lady, eighty-four years old, lying unconscious at the foot of the stairs. You go to the library to check an old newspaper and, sure enough, fifty years ago an eighty-four-year-old woman was pushed down the stairs by an intruder and died from the fall. Then there's stage three—*possession*—the influence on a person's activities by someone who's dead.''

Marritt waited until he was certain Racah had finished. ''And you believe in all that?''

''In sensitivity, yes.''

''What about haunting?''

''I do.''

''And possession?''

There was a pause.

''Quite frankly, Mr. Marritt, I'm a skeptic on the subject. But if one believes in sensitivity and haunting, it would be foolish to shut the door completely on possession.''

''You know something, doctor? I think it's a lot of crap.''

''Perhaps. But there are fairly well-documented instances of people without musical training sitting down and playing Mozart on the piano. Shakespeare paid quite a bit of attention to the parapsychological—witness the ghost of Hamlet's father and the premonitions of Caesar's wife. And the feats of truly great psychics like Croiset, Serios, and Daniel Dunglas Home are a matter of record. Still, if it makes you more content, fewer than one out of every million people is truly psychic. Most people who consider themselves endowed with extrasensory powers, aren't.

So the odds favor your initial hypothesis. The person you're seeking in connection with these murders is most likely, as you might put it, a nut.''

"Most likely a nut." Out on the street, the words ran through Marritt's mind. The possibility had been there from the beginning, but he was sure there was more to it than that. There was the money, and Klaus Ehrlich, and the deadly precision of three—maybe four—murders. And there was the music. Where did it come from? Who wrote it?

Marritt thought it was time to pay another visit on Judith Darr. But he'd have to wait a few hours—until near midnight.

Chapter 13

IT WAS ELEVEN O'CLOCK. The night was crisp and clear. Marritt and Judith stood at the edge of the plaza at Lincoln Center and looked in on Damrosch Park. Black marble benches were interspersed with travertine encasements that gleamed ghostly white. Hidden lamps set among the shrubs highlighted sycamore trees, turning their leaves a translucent green. A young couple speaking in muted tones sat nearby on one of the benches. Otherwise, the park was deserted.

"I'm scared," Judith whispered to Marritt. "Besides, I don't understand what you expect to get out of this."

"Don't argue," the detective told her. "You're Rebecca Morris. You know me as Klaus Ehrlich. You've made contact with David Hollister or Keith Swados—maybe both. Now you've been instructed to meet me here tonight, and you're worried. You need money and our little business venture, as Rebecca once put it, might be about to terminate."

Judith shivered.

"*Act it out!* Do it!" Suddenly, Marritt was Ehrlich. "Good evening, Miss Morris. It was good of you to come tonight. Follow me, please."

The detective turned. Judith followed.

"All right," Marritt said. "Ehrlich leads, but not into the park. Instead, he takes her down this corridor toward the back of the Opera House. Rebecca is getting scared. Ehrlich frightens her. But then, she sees David Hollister and Keith Swados by the hedge— right about . . . here."

Marritt stopped at the spot where the bodies had been discovered. The corridor was dark, with no one else in sight.

"You were to tell no one, Miss Morris. That was our agreement. Security has been breached."

Judith stared straight ahead.

"You have exchanged certain information," Marritt hissed. "I will ask you now—and I warn you, be very honest—have you discussed the project with anyone other than Mr. Hollister and Mr. Swados?"

"No."

"Only with each other?"

"That's right."

"Are you certain?"

"I swear it."

The detective moved closer. "How much do you know?"

"Nothing."

"How much do you know?"

"I know what you told me."

He was almost on top of her. "I ask you again, how much do you know?"

Judith fell backward against the hedge. "It's—it's Beethoven."

Slowly Marritt raised his index finger and pulled the trigger level with Judith's head. "That's it," he said. "Three people dead."

Judith stood, shaking. "You make it seem real."

"It is real. And it makes sense. Ehrlich finds a lost Beethoven manuscript. He takes it to Victor Pesage, and Pesage tells him to put together an orchestra. But somehow, David Hollister, Keith Swados, and Rebecca Morris compare notes. Now they can hear melody and harmony instead of just one part. It sounds like Beethoven. Maybe one of them manages to contact Ehrlich and asks the question. Maybe Ehrlich checks them out. Once suspicions surface, all three are eliminated. Then Ehrlich goes to their apartments to reclaim the music. The Stradivarius is lying there for the taking, so he takes it. Everything fits!"

"No, it doesn't," Judith said. "There's no motive."

"Motive! I'm a cop, and you're telling me about motive? Pesage and Ehrlich are putting together an orchestra."

"Then why not just go to the New York Philharmonic and say, 'I've found a symphony by Beethoven; play it.' Why does Karl Heiden have to disappear? And why the secrecy? Why not simply approach each musician and say, 'Here's ten thousand dollars; play Beethoven!' "

"I can feel it," Marritt said. "I feel it in my gut. Don't you see? Why does a thief steal a painting by Rembrandt, even though it can never be shown? Why do people do all the crazy things they do in this world? I'm telling you, we're dealing with someone who's putting together an orchestra to play Beethoven."

"Why Beethoven? Because a dead flutist put a question mark on her calendar next to his name? Or because a supposedly dead museum curator is involved? Lieutenant, Detective, or whatever it is I'm supposed to call you—I'm scared. Three people have been murdered, and I'm stuck in the middle while you go around play-acting. I can't stand it."

It had been a long day—and night.

"Come on," Marritt said, his voice softening. "I'll walk you home."

"And one thing more. My name is Judith. You don't have to keep calling me Miss Darr."

"All right. From now on, I'll call you Judith."
"And you?"
"Lieutenant will do nicely for now."

Just past midnight, they made their way along 87th Street, passing brownstone stoops. The sky was clear. As they neared Judith's building, their pace slowed.
"Would you do me a favor?"
"Sure," Marritt told her.
"I know it's late. But could you come upstairs and sit with me a while? I'm scared."
Marritt groaned—not audibly, but inside. He wanted to go home. As things stood, he'd be operating tomorrow on six hours' sleep. Now it looked like five.
"Please! I know you're tired, but I'm frightened. I don't want to be alone."
In a way, it was his fault that she was still involved. He was the one who'd manipulated her into staying on. He was the one who'd dragged her to Damrosch Park on a nightmarish journey through time. "All right," he told her. "But not for long."
They went upstairs to the fourth floor, and into Judith's apartment.
"Do you want some coffee?"
"Sure."
"Is Sanka okay? It's all I have."
"Sanka is fine."
When the water had come to a boil, Judith poured it into matching mugs, then handed one to Marritt, and settled down on the sofa. As he had done before, the detective sat in the chair by the door. Again, the

slats on the chair dug into his back the way they had the day he and Judith had met. Shifting position, he adjusted his shoulder holster, and the .38-caliber Smith & Wesson he wore became visible. Judith's eyes focused on the gun.

"There's something I'm curious about," Marritt told her. "I was doing some reading this morning. What's a clavier?"

She smiled. "It's an early keyboard instrument, like a piano or organ." Again, she eyed the weapon. "Do you always carry your gun?"

"All the time," Marritt told her. "Police regulations say we have to have it on duty. Off duty, I'm scared one of my kids will fool with it. I'd never leave it alone at home." Leaning back, he let his mind wander. "It's not easy for kids to have a father who's a cop. Not everyone thinks of policemen as honored individuals. And every time a newspaper headline says 'Cop Shot,' I wonder what it does to my kids' heads."

"Did you ever shoot anyone?"

"Once."

"What happened?"

"I killed him. It was sixteen years ago, up in Harlem. My partner and I busted a junkie in a tenement hall, and I went up to the roof to look for more. I found one. He pulled a knife. He was five feet away, and I froze. I'd never been in combat before. He wasn't moving. He just looked at me, and said, 'I'm gonna carve your heart out.' So I shot him. I didn't have to. According to the police manual, I was a step away from shooting. I could have told him to drop the knife, but I was scared and I was angry, and I blew him away. For a while, it bothered me, but I honestly believe the world's a better place for what I did.''

Judith didn't answer.

Marritt took a sip of coffee. He was tired and didn't want to talk about guns. ''What about you? If you don't mind my asking, how did you get involved with music?''

Judith's eyes took on a wistful, faraway look. ''Mostly, I think, it came from my father. He was a strange man. Very generous in some ways, very selfish in others. He died when I was seven, so I remember him as a figure of mythic proportions.''

''And?''

''He wasn't very good at sharing. Generosity was on his terms, or not at all. But I wanted to be loved and I took what was offered. Every Sunday afternoon, my father would lie on a chaise longue in the living room and listen to records—Mozart, Brahms, Beethoven. I'd come in, and if I was quiet he'd let me stay by his side and listen. It happened that way every Sunday afternoon. It was our own special time together. Now whenever I play, part of me plays for him. The music he loved most was Beethoven.''

''Why Beethoven?''

''That's something you'd find hard to understand. You have—'' She broke off, then began again. ''Two hundred years ago, something was ready to happen with music. Beethoven made it happen. He established music as a force capable of conveying a moral point of view. He went beyond anything that had been done musically before. Haydn wrote a hundred symphonies; Mozart, forty-one. Beethoven wrote nine, but they dwarf all the music the world has known. His Ninth Symphony was performed for the first time in Vienna in 1824. Beethoven was stone deaf, but the public didn't know. And because he was vain, he insisted on conducting. When the concert began, a conductor named Michael Umlauf stood to Beethoven's left, a little bit behind him. The orchestra and chorus had been told to follow Umlauf's lead and pay no attention at all to Beethoven. When the symphony ended, the audience broke into sustained applause. Beethoven heard nothing—and he was still conducting. He'd lost track of tempo and time. One of the chorus members stepped forward, touched his arm, and turned him around. Embarrassed, he realized the music was over, looked out at the audience, and bowed. And then, for the first time, the audience understood what was going on. They rose and cheered. They waved handkerchiefs and raised their arms. Three years later, when Beethoven died, all Vienna payed homage at his grave.''

Marritt sat silent, not wanting to rip Judith from her self-imposed trance. She had been transported to a place far away, long ago in time.

''If there is a Tenth Symphony,'' she said softly, ''it would be the most awesome discovery music has known.''

Chapter 14

WHATEVER THE VENTURE, whatever the plan, Americans were a problem. Carefully chosen, Europeans would perform properly. The Japanese were completely reliable. Americans were a different matter. He had opposed their inclusion from the start, but Pesage had insisted. And so, in his travels, he had evaluated and recruited Americans on the same basis as the others. Now it had been necessary to eliminate three of them, and the pity of it was that they had been quite talented. Their deaths were a tragedy, but necessary to the success of the larger plan. As for that other nettlesome matter, Pesage had endowed him with certain discretionary powers, and the violin had been there for the taking. Given the fact that morality reflects the whims of those in power, he had been fully justified in expropriating the Stradivarius. Adequate replacements for the three Americans had been found. All that remained were several "administrative" details, after which the project could proceed as planned.

Chapter 15

NINE A.M. The precinct house.

"Yesterday was a dark, dismal day in Queens," Marritt told Dema.

"What happened?"

"You name it. David's team lost in the Little League World Series. Jonathan cut his finger opening a can of tuna fish. And our car's transmission is gone forever. David and Jonathan will heal with time, but the transmission is dead. Twelve and a half years, we had that car. In another six months, it could have been Bar Mitzvahed.''

"You could take violin lessons,'' Dema offered. "Then maybe someone will come along and give you ten thousand dollars to buy a new car."

"Yeah, right. And maybe I'd wind up like David Hollister. No, thanks. One thing you learn fast on this job is there's no such thing as a free lunch. But since we're on the subject, what's happened lately?"

Methodical as always, Dema opened his expansion folder and scanned the previous day's notes. "I sent our copy of Judith Darr's music out for computer analysis. Some professor over at Juilliard has an ongoing project where pieces by Beethoven, Mozart, and Bach are being programmed into a computer. The idea is to determine which patterns make the music pleasing to the ears, or something like that. A by-product is that any piece can be fed into the computer for clues to authorship."

"And?"

"Karl Heiden's music is consistent with Beethoven. The problem is, Beethoven wrote in so many different styles that, one way or another, most music is consistent with Beethoven. At least that's how the people at the computer center see it."

"What about Pesage?"

"Nothing. The authorities in Austria say there's no basis for them to conduct an investigation until we provide evidence of wrongdoing on his part. And objectively speaking, nothing concrete links him to the murders. The official record says Karl Heiden is dead; and, even if Heiden is alive, his links to Pesage are tenuous.''

"Anything else?"

"No, sir."

Contemplating the task that lay ahead, Marritt rose from his desk. "All right," he told Dema. "Keep doing what you've been doing. If you need me, I'll be at the library at Lincoln Center."

The first floor of the library looked the same as before—less forbidding than the upper reaches, but hardly designed to make Marritt comfortable. Three rows of long wood tables ran adjacent to the west wall. A red-lettered sign nearby warned:

WHERE'S YOUR WALLET?

Many handbags and wallets have recently been stolen in this library. Please do not leave yours unattended. The library is not responsible for items that are lost or stolen.

Leaving the tables behind, Marritt journeyed to the second aisle, where the books on Beethoven were shelved. *Ein Wiener Beethoven Buch* ("No way," the detective told himself; "try another."). . . . *Beethoven im Kampfe mit dem Schicksal* ("Not so good either."). . . . At last, one in English —*Beethoven: Biography of a Genius,* by George R. Marek. Cradling the book in his hands, Marritt turned to the frontispiece and studied the portrait of the eighteenth-century composer inside. Powerfully built, clumsy and awkward; short, bull-shouldered. The face was marred by pockmarked skin; the features were prominent and strong with bushy brows above brilliant burning eyes and a broad forehead shadowed by unkempt hair. It was the visage of a man wholly lacking in physical grace, but vibrant and bold.

Turning to the text, Marritt began to read:

Beethoven grew from the soil of his times and stood deep in the cultural, political, and social streams that swirled around him. When he was eighteen, the French Revolution began. When he was twenty-two, the Reign of Terror in France made Europe tremble. When he was twenty-seven, Napoleon conquered Egypt. When he was forty-four, the Congress of Vienna redrew the map. When he was in his fifties, the Monroe Doctrine was proclaimed, the first railroad began to chug in England, and the Industrial Revolution was hurrying on.

The book was readable! If he took his time, there was nothing in it that Marritt couldn't understand. What else was on the shelves? *Beethoven und die Dichtung* ("Forget that one!"). . . . *Beethoven*, by Maynard Solomon ("Maybe."). . . . *Ludwig Beethoven*, by Fischer and Kock. . . . *Beethoven—The Last Decade*, by Martin Cooper. More confident than before, the detective gathered a half dozen books and reached into his pocket for a small notepad. In nineteen years as a cop, he'd reconstructed thousands of lives. There was no reason he couldn't penetrate the world of Beethoven.

Judith put down the viola and looked at her watch. It was almost noon. She'd been practicing for three hours. Sometimes she thought she'd be better off throwing in the towel and auditioning for the New York Philharmonic. The next time an orchestra member quit or retired, she could walk into the audition and help herself to a thirty-thousand-dollar-a-year job. In time, with seniority, she'd earn even more. No more scrounging around for performance bookings; no more financial binds. But knowing herself, she knew she wouldn't do it. She would succeed on her own terms, or not at all. That meant endless hours of practice and concentration—except that it was hard to concentrate with everything that was going on. Her mind kept drifting off to Beethoven.

In 1884, a cantata had been found with Beethoven's name inscribed on page 1. Beethoven had been dead for fifty-seven years. Amidst a whirl of excitement, the music was brought to the great Johannes Brahms, who told the world, "Even if there were no name on the title page, none other could be conjectured. Through and through, the music is Beethoven."

But that had been a century ago; and the cantata had been composed by the young Beethoven. Nothing resembling a mature symphony to complement the first nine had ever been suggested, much less found.

Judith picked up her viola and began to play again.

Six P.M. The library was closing. Marritt gathered up his books and notes, and wondered whether or not to go home. David and Jonathan would be watching television or fighting or doing something to make noise. If he wanted to concentrate, it made sense to go back to the precinct house instead.

He had spent seven hours in the library. What had he learned? That Beethoven wrote symphonies, operas, overtures, sonatas, masses, cantatas, ballets, concertos, string quartets, and something called lieder; that Beethoven's music did a lot of sudden, unexpected things; that Beethoven "composed like Beethoven and no one else"; that he was a "master of passions," an "architect of daring, suitable to the new world." As Beethoven aged, Marritt now knew, he had grown suspicious, cantankerous, and quarrelsome, given to fits of rage. As deafness took hold, he had fallen into a world of his own. Passersby on the street would stop and stare at the strange, unkempt man, mumbling, sometimes shouting musical sounds. Servants talked of hearing the master behind closed doors singing, banging, stamping his feet at all hours. Yet from that pained, tormented mind flowed music thought by many to be man's best hope for communing with the Gods.

Back at the precinct house, Marritt telephoned home to say he'd be working late; then settled behind his desk alone, taking notes, writing everything down. In Vienna, Beethoven had been welcomed initially for his virtuoso piano skills. His powerful playing contrasted with the more delicate style then in vogue. He ate heartily and drank great quantities of wine, but was seldom inebriated. "Not that it has anything to do with solving three murders," the detective grumbled. Maybe he should ditch it all and go home. What time was it? Not quite seven. He might as well read on a little longer.

More note-taking—mostly describing Beethoven's music: "Beethoven identified with the common man. Mozart wrote for courts and kings; Beethoven wrote for the world." Then Marritt copied a description of the Fifth Symphony from one of the library tomes:

> The sky is huge and black, but there comes a tiny point of light. As it expands with frightening speed and mounting energy, we do not know whether to hope or to fear—until the whole universe is abruptly ablaze.

Next, the Heiligenstadt Testament. What the hell was that? He shouldn't have skimmed the last chapter. Go back and read it through. The first signs of deafness appeared in 1798, when Beethoven was twenty-eight years old. In vain, he consulted innumerable physicians. The state of the art was quackery, nothing more—rubbing ointment on his arms; applying herbs to his stomach. "To be forced to become a philosopher when one is only twenty-eight years old," Beethoven wrote, "—it is hard." Three years later, Beethoven confided by letter to a friend. "My most prized possession, my hearing, has greatly deteriorated. My ears continue to hum and buzz day and night. . . . In the theater, I have to place myself close to the orchestra in order to understand what the actor is saying. . . . I cannot hear the high notes of instruments or voices. Sometimes I can scarcely hear a person who speaks softly. I can hear sounds, but cannot make out the words. . . . It is surprising that some people have never noticed my deafness; but since I have always been liable to fits of absentmindedness, they attribute my hardness of hearing to that. . . . I beg you to treat what I have told you about my hearing as a great secret to be trusted to no one.''

Marritt read on, transported back in time.

''A musician can hear music without hearing. In his mind, he knows what those silent sounds on paper will sound like when they come to life. . . . No happiness exists from without; I must create everything myself in my mind. . . . I will seize Fate by the throat. It shall certainly not bend and crush me.''

And then, the Testament, written at Beethoven's summer retreat in Heiligenstadt; dated October 6, 1802, when Beethoven was thirty-two years old:

For my brothers Carl and Johann: To be read and executed after my death—

My fellow men, who consider me unfriendly, peevish, or even misanthropic, how greatly you do me wrong. For you do not know the secret reason why I appear to be so. Ever since childhood, my heart and soul have been imbued with the tender feeling of goodwill. . . .

But for the last six years I have been afflicted with an incurable complaint. From year to year, my hopes of being cured have been shattered, and finally I have been forced to accept the prospect of a permanent infirmity. . . . Yet I cannot bring myself to say to people, "Speak up, shout, for I am deaf." Alas! How can I possibly refer to the impairment of a sense which in me should be more perfectly developed than in other people, a sense which at one time I possessed in the greatest perfection. . . . I cannot do it. . . . I must live quite alone and may creep into society only as often as sheer necessity demands. I must live like an outcast. If I appear in company, I am overcome by a burning anxiety, a fear that I am running the risk of letting people notice my condition. . . . How humiliated I have felt when somebody standing beside me heard the sound of a flute in the distance and I heard nothing, when somebody heard a shepherd sing and again I heard nothing. Such experiences made me despair, and I was on the point of putting an end to my life. The only thing that held me back was my art. For indeed, it seems impossible to leave this world before I have produced all the works that I feel the urge to compose, and thus I have dragged on this miserable existence. . . . I hope that I shall persist in my resolve to endure to the end, until it pleases the inexorable Parcae to cut the thread. . . . Almighty God, who looks down on my innermost soul, you see into my heart and know that it is filled with love for humanity and a desire to do good. My fellow men, when someday you read this statement, remember that you have done me wrong. . . .

Laying the book aside, Marritt rubbed his eyes. It was eleven o'clock, time to go home. What a world! He felt sorry for Beethoven.

Judith turned back the covers on her bed, and wondered if she wasn't too self-critical. She was always down on herself for something. Either this piece wasn't sufficiently polished, or that composition didn't flow. The least she could do was learn to distinguish between things that did and didn't matter.

Coming up, she had a recital scheduled for mid-October. That was important. A lot of critics and patrons would be there. If she performed well, major bookings could follow. And then there was Ehrlich's project—an unknown performance at an unknown site for reasons she couldn't begin to understand. She should never have taken the money. But if she'd said no, maybe she'd have wound up like Arnold Buxton, crushed in an elevator. Who knew which course was more likely to bring her out alive? And the irony of it all was that, even if she survived, she'd wind up in trouble—because she'd earned every penny of that ten thousand dollars, and there was no way she was going to pay taxes on it. But the Internal Revenue Service wouldn't see it that way. If they found out about it—and probably they would—somehow they'd fuck her over.

Another day. Sitting at his desk in the precinct house, Marritt began to read.

Beethoven rose every morning at dawn and, after coffee, went directly to his private study. Whatever the season, he took a mid-morning walk, composing as he went, before going back to his desk. Dinner at two; a long walk, again composing; drinks at a nearby tavern; evening meal. He was in bed by ten.

Unlike Mozart, Beethoven composed slowly, working on several pieces at a time. "His Symphonies," wrote one scholar, "form a series of peaks, each with its own characteristic features—clefts, glaciers, descending torrents and majestic waterfalls, sunny uplands and shining lakes."

Torrents. Glaciers. Marritt looked down at his notes. They consisted mostly of quotations and book excerpts. Leafing back through the data he'd gathered, he groped for a formula that would bring organization and order. When were the Beethoven symphonies written? What were they about? He needed a chart. For most of the morning, the detective labored at his new task. By noon, a chart was in working order:

BEETHOVEN'S SYMPHONIES

First Symphony
Completed in 1799
First performed on April 2, 1800
A traditional eighteenth-century work: light, pleasant, charming, good-humored.

Second Symphony
Completed in 1802
First performed on April 5, 1803
Joyous, bold. "The work of a mature master who is settling acounts with the high-classic symphonic tradition before embarking on an unprecedented musical voyage."

Third Symphony
Completed in 1804
First performed on April 7, 1805
The ultimate musical definition of heroism; a clear departure from the classical mold. Originally written to honor Napoleon, but Beethoven grew angry with Napoleon's dictatorial ways. The dedication was withdrawn. "To some, the symphony was maddeningly incomprehensible, frightening. To others, it was altogether thrilling, a new galaxy of music in which constellations moved in bold new patterns and dizzying motion."

Fourth Symphony
Completed in 1806
First performed in March 1807

"Shit," the detective muttered. There was no descriptive passage on his chart for the Fourth Symphony. He'd come back to that.

Fifth Symphony
Completed in 1807
First performed on December 22, 1808
Written over a three-year period with many preliminary sketches and changes. The first movement is a struggle between darkness and light; the last, a majestic hymn to victory. The symphony is thought to represent a duel between free will and determinism. Of the four-note opening, Beethoven once said, "Thus Fate knocks at the door."

Sixth Symphony
Completed in 1808
First performed on December 22, 1808 (the same day as the Fifth)
Known as "The Pastoral Symphony"

Beethoven identified its five movements as follows: (1) Pleasant cheerful feelings aroused on approaching the countryside; (2) Scene by a brook; (3) Jolly gathering of villagers; (4) Thunderstorm; (5) Shepherd's song—grateful thanks to the Almighty after the storm.

Seventh Symphony
Completed in 1812
First performed on December 8, 1813
Moves even further away from the traditional classical mold; written simultaneously with the Eighth.

Eighth Symphony
Completed in 1812
First performed on February 27, 1814

Once again, there was no descriptive entry on the detective's chart. He'd have to brush up on Beethoven's Eighth.

Ninth Symphony
Completed in 1823
First performed on May 7, 1824
A mighty hymn of praise and thanksgiving, honoring the Brotherhood of Man and the Fatherhood of God. The bulk of the Ninth Symphony was written in 1823. However, the theme from its second movement is found in an 1815 sketchbook, and the first movement dates from 1817. Beethoven began serious work on the symphony in 1822. It has a choral ending and four movements: (1) struggle; (2) humor; (3) contemplation; (4) jubilation.

Laying the chart aside, Marritt checked his watch. It was time for lunch. A cheeseburger and Coke would do nicely. An hour later, he was back at work. In mid-afternoon, Dema dropped by to report "no progress" on the case. Someone from the Commissioner's office called for an update. Then Marritt returned to his books.

Beethoven's personal life saw little joy. Though often "in love," he never married, moving from one unfulfilling relationship to another. Almost always, he was the party scorned, losing in the end to more suitable lovers. In 1815, his brother Caspar died, leaving a widow, Johanna, and a nine-year-old son, Karl. Beethoven sought exclusive guardianship of the child, claiming that Johanna was an unfit mother. Five years later, after bitter legal proceedings, the composer emerged victorious, but the victory was hollow. Karl attempted suicide, recovered, and embarked upon a military career, refusing to have anything more to do with his uncle. The entire affair left Beethoven, who had been seeking a "son," tormented and shattered.

Then came deafness. Like a deadly mist, the silence fell, leaving him isolated and even more alone. As the condition obliterated all worldly sounds, Beethoven took to offering bound memorandum pads to visitors. All of their comments were written down. He, in turn, would answer orally, except when discussing a private matter in a public place. On Beethoven's death in 1827, four hundred "Conversation Books" were found. Of those, two-thirds were destroyed by his contemporary and biographer, Anton Schindler.

Schindler? Who the hell was Schindler? Again, Marritt had paid the price for skimming chapters. He decided to go back and check the biographical glossary in one of the books. *Salieri; Schenk;* here it was—

Anton Felix Schindler
(1795-1864)
Devoted "slave" of Beethoven during the last twelve years of the composer's life. Wrote biography, published in 1840.

Schindler! The name had a classic sound. He might even be an interesting character to read about, but not now. It was six o'clock and Marritt's wife would have a fit if he worked late again. Better to save Schindler for tomorrow.

Sometimes she was too devoted to her professional life. Judith knew that; at least, that was what friends told her. She should work less; date more. Except she was never quite sure whom to date. Everyone was anonymous in New York. There was no way to meet this person next door or that one down the street. Involvements with other musicians scared her. They were her friends, but seldom worked as lovers. She'd tried—many times; but somehow the relationships never evolved. Not that she wasn't desirable. Her body was outstanding if anyone took the time to look, and her face was kind of pretty. Maybe she was searching for a father figure, which was why her affairs with contemporaries never lasted.

The top of her dresser needed dusting. So did the stereo cabinet and shelves. In another hour, she'd stop practicing and break for dinner; then maybe clean up the apartment or go to a movie. All her life, Judith had been self-sufficient, but Klaus Ehrlich had put an end to that. Now she needed someone to protect her and promise that everything would be all right.

Another morning, and the same pile of books. Marritt settled behind his desk, ready to work.

"Beethoven freed music," wrote one scholar. "He captured sounds, heavenly and infernal. His music inspires awe, fear, happiness, and pain; solemnity, ecstacy, suffering, and grandeur; torment, yearning, darkness, and joy."

"That was quite a list," the detective noted. Leafing through the book, he came to a portrait of Beethoven, drawn when the composer was fifty-four years old. The hands were remarkable; thick-veined and strong. The face was tormented. The eyes still burned. "In the Ninth Symphony," the book continued, "Beethoven writes of a creator who dwells above the stars. It is the most universally appealing musical work known to man."

More books. The task continued: "Beethoven was fortified in courage by the Enlightenment. The time was receptive. It was ready to welcome a genius who broke precedent. "Beethoven's *Fidelio* was a failure when first performed, but was later revived to critical acclaim. . . . Beethoven's first sketches for what eventually became the Ninth Symphony appear on loose leaves dated 1815. *In 1818, he began to plan for two symphonies to appear together.*"

Marritt stopped; then read the sentence through a second time. ". . . *two symphonies to appear together.*" Numbers nine—and ten? The book went on: "In 1819, Beethoven ceased work on the Ninth Symphony and turned to the *Missa Solemnis,* his major religious work. The mass was completed in 1823 and performed for the first time in 1824."

Nothing more on the symphony to appear with number nine, only the vaguest mention of a "plan." There had to be more. Yet here the book returned to Schindler:

Anton Felix Schindler was born in Moravia on June 13, 1795. His father, a local schoolmaster, was a good amateur musician, and Shindler received early training on the violin. In 1813 at age eighteen, he journeyed to Vienna to study law. The following year, he was asked by an acquaintance to deliver a note to Beethoven, who received the young man casually but in a manner that was kind.

Marritt read on. Soon after his encounter with Beethoven, Schindler took a job clerking for an attorney who, by more than chance, was Beethoven's personal counselor. Meanwhile, the casual first meeting led to ties that blossomed. In time, Schindler passed his law examinations, but his principal chore became serving Beethoven. He was The Great One's private secretary without pay—a servile, self-seeking flatterer, who ran errands, handled correspondence, and otherwise performed at Beethoven's command. Meanwhile, Beethoven treated him with mounting scorn, and worship mingled with hatred in Schindler's veins. Then, in 1824, the two men quarreled bitterly over the first public performance of the Ninth Symphony. Schindler supervised the administrative work that went into its staging, and while the event was a brilliant success artistically, financially it failed. Beethoven accused Schindler of embezzling some of the receipts, and banished him from his service. "An obtrusive appendix; a miserable rogue," Beethoven called him. Schindler pleaded for reconciliation as "a friend." Soon after, Beethoven penned a response:

> As for friendship, that is a difficult thing in your case. I learned some time ago to know you from a side which is not to your credit. And I must confess that the purity of my character does not permit me to recompense mere favors with friendship. I entrust you to come no more until I send for you.

Marritt turned to the following page, and stared at a portrait of Anton Schindler. He was posed by a pillar, standing in formal attire. The eyes were cold and very hard. Thin pursed lips; rimless glasses. There was nothing about him the detective liked. For a good five minutes, Marritt studied the portrait; then read on:

"Beethoven's music is characterized by power and emotion. . . . Beethoven did not think in words or formulated precepts. He thought in sound. . . ." An entry in Beethoven's diary declared, "All evil is mysterious and appears greatest when viewed in solitude." Then came reference to the choral finale of Beethoven's Ninth:

> Above the starry canopy
> There must dwell a loving Father
> World, do you know your Creator
> Above the stars, must He dwell.

At one o'clock, the detective broke for lunch. Forty minutes later, he was back with his books. Beethoven's final months were marked by weakness and ill-health. His mind remained capable of brilliant creation but, at age fifty-six, he was no longer physically able to write. More than ever, he was isolated and alone. At last, on his deathbed, he called for Schindler. And, as though the years had never passed, the sycophant lay servile again before the master.

On the afternoon of March 26, 1827, with Beethoven's death imminent, Schindler accompanied Beethoven's boyhood friend, Stephan von Breuning, to the Währing parish cemetery to select an appropriate gravesite. As night approached, a sudden storm forced them to seek shelter in a nearby village. When they returned home after dark, Beethoven was dead.

For several days, the great man lay in state as a procession of mourners passed by. A pyramidal stone was prepared for his grave: "BEETHOVEN: Rejoice in thy eternity!" On the day of burial, twenty thousand of his countrymen stood silent as Franz Grillparzer delivered the funeral oration:

> You have not lost him; you have won him. No living man enters the halls of the immortals. Not until the body has perished do their portals open. He whom you mourn stands from now onward among the great of all ages, inviolate forever. Return homeward, therefore, in sorrow yet resigned. And should you ever in times to come feel the overpowering might of his creations like an onrushing storm, remember this hour . . .

It was 7:00 P.M. Marritt was hungry. An auxiliary cop brought in a sandwich from a deli nearby. Ham and swiss on rye, with lettuce, and lots of mustard. Marritt hadn't read this much since high school; maybe not even then.

The day after Beethoven died, Schindler and Von Breuning went to his room in search of several bank notes Beethoven had willed to his nephew, Karl. They couldn't find them. That afternoon, they returned with Karl Holz—one of Beethoven's last friends. A battered cabinet stood on the floor. Holz pulled at a nail protruding from its frame, and a secret drawer was revealed. Inside, with the bank notes, were three items: the Heiligenstadt Testament; Beethoven's diary for the years 1812 through 1818; and a letter in Beethoven's hand, dated July 6–7, year unknown, addressed to "Immortal Beloved." The identity of the woman was to remain forever unknown.

At Von Breuning's insistence, the diary and letters were forwarded to proper hands. Schindler lay claim to all else that lay unguarded, and later sold the majority of Beethoven's belongings to the King of Prussia for a lifetime annuity. Of the 400 Conversation Books that fell into his possession, 264 were destroyed. Their eradication, Schindler maintained, was necessary to protect Beethoven's reputation, for they contained entries that were in some cases "trivial" and, in others, "politically undesirable." A footnote at the bottom of the page concluded the saga:

In 1977, at the Beethoven Congress in Berlin, hand-writing analysts confirmed that Schindler had entered approximately one hundred fifty of his comments in the Conversation Books *after* Beethoven died. No motive for these after-the-fact entries has been found.

Closing the book, Marritt pondered the issues at hand. Now that he had direction, the next step was to consolidate his find.

The hour was late. Judith had brushed her teeth and put up her hair. She had planned to go to sleep, but now there was this crazy cop at her door asking if she had any recordings of symphonies by Beethoven.

"I'm on to something," Marritt told her. "I want you to play Beethoven for me. And then I want you to explain what it is that makes his symphonies great."

Chapter 16

MARRITT SAT ON THE SOFA. Judith was wearing a sleeveless nightgown—white cotton with ribbon trim, an eyelet pattern around the neck. The detective didn't seem to notice. He wasn't in the habit of visiting witnesses late at night, but he was on a roll and determined not to lose it.

"Don't you understand? We're investigating a crime that took place in 1827, when Beethoven died. It's there. Everything fits!"

Judith waited, not knowing what to expect next.

Marritt forged ahead.

"Beethoven writes a Tenth Symphony. It's his masterpiece, his final gift. Maybe he dictates the music to Schindler while he's dying. Maybe Schindler finds it in the room after Beethoven is dead. Either way, Schindler gets control of the manuscript. He hates Beethoven. For years, he's envied and despised him. Now, with Beethoven gone, Schindler can perpetrate the ultimate treachery. So what does he do? He can't sell the music, because that would give Beethoven his monument. Maybe he contemplates holding the symphony and trying to pass it off as his own years later. But that's unrealistic, and he knows it; the music is instantly recognizable as Beethoven. Only one option is left—destroy the symphony. But Schindler can't bring himself to do it; the music is too magnificent. He's in a quandary. He doesn't know what to do, but one thing is certain—the Conversation Books contain too many clues, too many allusions to a Tenth Symphony; so Schindler goes through the books and burns them. He should probably burn them all, but he's greedy and the books that are left can be sold for a healthy sum. Eventually, Schindler dies, his dilemma unresolved. A century later, Karl Heiden becomes curator of the Beethoven Museum in Bonn. He's an archivist, a scholar. He finds one clue, then another. Finally, the Tenth Symphony falls into his hands. Heiden has the most valuable and potentially the most sought-after piece of music the world has ever known. Now he's the one who wants money, so he goes to Victor Pesage, and Pesage tells him to put together an orchestra. After that, your guess is as good as mine.''

Judith sat silent, fighting to retain her composure. ''Why do you want me to play Beethoven for you now?''

''Because I want to understand what it is about Beethoven's music that makes people do the things they do. And you're the only person I know who can make me understand.''

There was a pause.

''All right. Give me a minute to put some clothes on.''

Close to midnight, they began. Judith took a gold-trimmed box from her collection of records.

Marritt watched. ''Which symphony are you starting with?''

''The Sixth.''

''Why not the First?''

''Because I feel like listening to the Sixth.''

With the detective still sitting on the sofa, she slid a disc onto the turntable. The tone arm dropped. ''This is the *Pastoral* Symphony,'' she said as the first notes sounded. ''According to Beethoven, each movement signifies an image encountered during a day in the country. It starts with the cheerful, joyous emotions Beethoven felt on reaching the countryside.''

Marritt listened. The melody seemed ordinary. At one point, the music built toward a crescendo, but then it dropped off just when he was getting interested.

''Imagine yourself outdoors,'' Judith prodded.

"There's an open sky; you feel grass against your feet."

"Why grass?"

"Because you're imaginative."

The movement lasted twelve minutes. Marritt looked around the room as time passed. The furniture was secondhand, mostly cheap. Numerous personal touches were evident in photos of Judith's parents and miscellaneous memorabilia but, obviously, a sparse existence was the price of her art.

"This is the second movement," the detective heard her saying. "Beethoven is standing at the edge of a brook. Listen, and you'll hear the melody repeat."

Marritt liked the way it sounded, the way it grew. Then it vanished.

"How come it's a brook?"

"Because Beethoven said so."

The second movement was a bit shorter than the first. Toward the end, Marritt's thoughts wandered. Again, he looked around the room before focusing on Judith. She was wearing a blue cotton skirt with an American Indian design embroidered in yellow and red thread. Thinking back to the way she'd looked in the nightgown a half-hour earlier, he realized that this was the first time he'd seen her legs.

Concentrate on the music! The third movement began—a "jolly gathering of villagers," it had said on his chart.

"Beethoven originated the concept of unity between symphony movements," Judith announced. "And within a movement, he'll start very small and let an idea grow in size to enormous proportions. Then, suddenly, he'll drop you off a cliff. There's a good example of that in the thunderstorm ahead.''

"How can you have a thunderstorm in a symphony?"

"You're being stubborn," she said. "Just relax; listen to the music."

More melody, a little tedious. Then, slowly, little violin raindrops. Tiny at first, they began picking up strength. Then an undercurrent of drums. More drums, horns—and suddenly, a towering storm was raging.

"Do you hear it? Do you hear the storm?"

Frightening, violent music sounded. Driving rain fell in torrents. A piccolo shrieked above the chaos. Lightning flared; thunder rolled; the heavens raged. And then, as suddenly as it had begun, the storm faded. The rain grew soft. A shepherd's song was heard—a simple melody begun by a flute, repeated by horns; then violins giving grateful thanks to the Almighty again and again, until the whole orchestra sounded. The sun was ablaze. The melody faded, returned, crescendoed ever louder, each time fuller, richer, more magnificent than before. And then, the symphony was over, and Judith was sitting by Marritt's side asking, "Now do you understand?"

The detective nodded. "That last part was really beautiful."

She smiled. "Come back again. Next time we'll listen to Beethoven's Ninth."

"I'd like that."

Again the smile, warmer this time. "Lieutenant, can I ask you something?"

"Sure."

"I feel silly, calling you 'Lieutenant' all the time. Would a first name be all right?"

"My name is Richard. I guess you know that."

They said goodnight, awkwardly shaking hands. Marritt was rather proud of himself; he had listened to Beethoven. Somehow the music would make the subway ride home a little shorter. But as he left Judith's apartment and walked out into the night, a thought that went beyond music and beyond three murders was preying on his mind. He was aware of the fact that his feelings for Judith Darr had crossed over the line between police work and caring. He liked her, liked being with her, liked watching her face as the music played.

In nineteen years as a cop, Richard Marritt had always kept his nose clean. In twelve years of marriage, he had never entertained the notion of an affair—until now.

Chapter 17

MARRITT SAT AT THE KITCHEN TABLE, giving "grateful thanks to the Almighty" that he had the day off from work.

The subway ride home from Judith Darr's had lasted forever. He hadn't gotten to sleep until three o'clock. Now, over a breakfast of scrambled eggs and bacon, he was looking across the table at his wife. When Jonathan was born, she'd quit her job to devote herself full time to motherhood. Now, ten years later, she was considering going back to work.

Their marriage was comfortable, held together by the children and a genuine caring for one another. Viewed in the light of day, the idea of a liaison with Judith Darr made the detective feel more than a little guilty.

"Did you see the newspaper this morning?" Marritt asked. "There's an article on cab drivers in New York. All they need for a hack license is medical authorization, a social security number, and twenty-two out of thirty right answers on a multiple-choice test. The City doesn't even give them a road test to find out if they can drive safely or not." Spreading some butter on a piece of toast, he continued his report. "Half of the cabbies can't find an address outside of Manhattan. God forbid you should need a ride to Staten Island or the Bronx. A lot of them have trouble speaking English—they're Iranian or Haitian or something like that."

The telephone rang, and the detective's wife got up from the table to answer it. Marritt finished his toast and added his plate to those already in the kitchen sink. Just for a moment, the "Shepherd's Song" from the night before passed through his thoughts. It was odd how the melody was there without any conscious effort to recall it. Five weeks ago, who would have thought he'd be humming Beethoven? But five weeks ago, it had been the end of August. Now it was October fourth. A lot had happened in those five weeks. And the period beginning November 4 through November 9 was just one month away.

Judith stood where she so often stood—in front of the mirror with her viola. Two weeks from now, an audience of patrons, critics, and friends would be at her recital. It was important that she be good—better than good. Talent and discipline were the minimum prerequisites for a classical musician to stand a chance of making it to the top.

The program she'd chosen was varied, maybe even a little eclectic. Bach's Suite in G Major; Brahms' Opus 120—those were standard. But mixed in were Benjamin Britten's "Lachrymae" and Suite No. 1 by Max Reger. For a while, she'd considered adding Beethoven's "Serenade," but decided against it. She wanted her mind free from fear on recital night. Nothing could eliminate the butterflies that came with performing, but she didn't need a piece by Beethoven as an onstage reminder of Klaus Ehrlich. Beethoven could wait; she'd get to him in November. Anyway, that was what Marritt thought. Judith thought the whole idea was crazy. Forget about logic, she told herself. Forget about everything you've ever read. Be inquisitive and go for an intuitive, gut reaction. The viola part to Klaus Ehrlich's music—was it Beethoven?

Maybe.

Dinner was over; the kids were in bed. Marritt was on edge. The case had him hooked. No way was he

going to take tomorrow off. All day, while he'd
puttered around the house, visions of Schindler had
danced in his head. If that son of a bitch from the
past was going to dominate his mind, at the very
least the detective would be paid overtime for it. First
thing in the morning, Marritt planned on being at the
library at Lincoln Center.

The evening passed. It was a cool night. Marritt
was up at six o'clock. By eight, he was at Lincoln
Center.

The library was closed—open at 10:00 A.M., a
sign posted on the outer door read. Cursing, the
detective gave the door a sharp kick, then moved
across the street to a neighborhood coffee shop. Two
hours later, after reading the *Times* and the *News,* he
went back to the library and proceeded to the Beethoven shelf. . . . *Beethoven and the World of Music,*
by Manuel Komroff. . . . *Goethe und Beethoven,* by
Richard Benz. The detective knew what he wanted.
Here it was—*Beethoven As I Knew Him,* by Anton
Felix Schindler.

Opening the book, Marritt skimmed through the
Editor's Foreword and a brief biographical sketch of
Schindler, then turned to the text itself. "Ludwig van
Beethoven," the book began, "was born in Bonn on
17 December 1770. His father, Johann van Beetho-
ven, was a tenor in the Electoral choir, and died in
Bonn in 1792. His mother . . ."

In pedestrian fashion the tome went on, detailing
Beethoven's early life. After reading the first fifty or
so pages, Marritt skipped to a chapter entitled, "1815

to Beethoven's Death." There, Schindler's account of his own first meeting with Beethoven was reported:

> In the winter of 1813-14, a well-to-do music lover by the name of Pettenkoffer assembled a group of young people in his home to play orchestral music every Saturday. I was a member of the group and, at such a gathering toward the end of March, one of the musicians asked me to deliver a note to Beethoven. Joyfully, I accepted the assignment. And so it was that my desire to stand for a moment in the presence of the great man whose works had inspired me was unexpectedly fulfilled. The next morning, with pounding heart, I climbed the stairs to Beethoven's house and was admitted by a servant who led me to The Master, busy at his desk. Beethoven read the note, and the audience was over. This incident was the most important thing that had ever happened in the life of this poor student and the unlooked-for beginning of a close relationship.

"Bullshit," muttered the detective. "Unlooked-for beginning, my ass."

The book went on. It was a self-serving work, glorifying Schindler for his relationship with "The Master" as much as it glorified Beethoven. Only once did it strike a poignant note—a recollection of Beethoven's futile attempt to conduct the dress rehearsal of his opera *Fidelio* at a time when deafness had overcome him:

> We all advised against it. In fact, we pleaded with him to resist his desires and remember the difficulties that had attended previous concerts. Finally, after several days of indecision, he declared his readiness to conduct the work. At his request, I accompanied him to the

dress rehearsal. The E major overture went perfectly for, despite his hesitations, the members of the orchestra moved in their customary disciplined ranks. But in the very first number, it was apparent that Beethoven could hear nothing of what was happening on stage. He seemed to hold back. The orchestra stayed with him, but the singers pressed on and everything fell apart. There was general confusion. The musicians were stopped. The impossibility of continuing under the direction of the creator of the work was obvious. But who was to tell him? Who was to say, "It cannot be done; go away, you unhappy man!" Beethoven grew apprehensive and turned from one side to the other, searching the faces to see what had interrupted the rehearsal. Then he called me to his side and handed me his notebook, motioning for me to write down what was wrong. I inscribed, "Please don't go on; I'll explain at home." Without stopping, he hastened to his apartment. Once there, he threw himself onto the sofa, covered his face with both hands, and remained so until dinner. During the meal, he did not say a word. His whole demeanor bespoke depression and defeat.

By mid-afternoon, Marritt had finished the book. Schindler had covered his tracks well. There were no clues to lend credence to the existence of a Tenth Symphony. Gathering his notes, the detective left the library and walked north to the 20th Precinct station house. When he arrived, Dema was reviewing the case file in the upstairs office.

"Long time no see," the detective offered. "What's happening?"

"The usual," Dema answered. "No real clues. I looked into the Beethoven Museum in Bonn. During

Karl Heiden's tenure as curator, its collection expanded to three thousand books and ten thousand newspaper and magazine articles—all about Beethoven. As far as Victor Pesage is concerned, there's no new information, but I did come across one oddity. Beethoven died in March 1827. Pesage was born in March 1927—exactly one hundred years later.''

"And?"

Dema shrugged. "And nothing. It's probably a coincidence, but I thought it was worth mentioning."

Marritt did some quick mental arithmetic. Schindler had died in 1864. That was thirty-seven years after Beethoven. Karl Heiden was forty-two. That meant he was born in. . . . The numbers were a jumble. There was no sense in pursuing them.

"I've been listening to Beethoven," the detective said, shifting the conversation. "I'm not sure what that accomplishes, but it's made life more interesting. The problem is, the more questions I answer about the case, the more new ones come up. Like, why was it necessary for the musicians to be recruited in secret? Why did Karl Heiden have to disappear?"

Dema waited. Marritt continued.

"I keep coming back to Schindler. He's the linchpin for it all. He and Von Breuning were the first people to arrive after Beethoven's death. Then Von Breuning died two months later. That gave Schindler a clear field for whatever he intended. Things seem to fit, but then I tell myself, 'Hold on, we're in the twentieth century. Stop looking backward; concentrate on now!' '' Marritt was thinking out loud, not sure what to do next. "Jim, do me a favor, will you? When you get a chance, see if Victor Pesage has a history as an orchestra conductor; the same for Heiden.''

Dema began to answer, but the telephone interrupted.

Marritt picked up the receiver. "Hello! . . . What's the matter?'' A look of concern crossed his face. "All right. I'll be right over.''

Judith stood in the doorway to her apartment. One look told Marritt that she was terrified. Somehow, the passage of time had made Klaus Ehrlich seem less real to her. Now, again, Ehrlich was a reality.

"Where is it?''

"Inside, on the dresser,'' she answered.

"How was it delivered?''

"By mail.''

Taking her arm, Marritt led the way inside. There, on the dresser, was a plain sheet of paper with a neatly typed note:

Dear Miss Darr,

My best wishes to you for your upcoming recital on the 18th of this month.

Please do not neglect your other music. Travel plans will be sent to you shortly before the November 4 departure date.

Kindest regards,
Klaus Ehrlich

"Do you have the envelope?"

Judith pointed to a plain white wrapper, postmarked New York. Like the message, the address had been typed.

"What's this about a recital?"

"It's a concert I'm giving." Her voice trembled as it had when Marritt confronted her on the day they'd met. "I—it's at the New School, on October eighteenth."

Marritt stared at the note. "I guess this is Klaus Ehrlich's way of letting you know he has an eye on you," he said at last. "We'll check it for fingerprints, but there won't be any."

Chapter 18

SOMETIMES COPS GET LUCKY. Every now and then, inspired thinking adds a point or two. But Marritt knew that police work was ninety percent perspiration, which meant that no stone could be left unturned. The following morning, he was at the fingerprint lab when the day shift started.

Half a dozen technicians were on duty. Nodding hello to each of them, the detective gravitated toward Danny Keegan, a heavyset, balding man he'd known since their rookie days together nineteen years earlier. Keegan was the sort of person who'd talk all day if you let him. He was also the best fingerprint expert Marritt knew.

"Well, if it ain't Mr. Celebrity," Keegan observed as the detective came into view. "I've been reading about you in the newspapers lately."

For the next few minutes, Marritt indulged his former partner in small talk, then reached into the folder he was carrying, and drew out a clear plastic envelope with Klaus Ehrlich's letter inside.

"Don't tell me the famous Richard Marritt has a clue!"

"Danny, cut the crap and tell me what the chances are of getting a print off this piece of paper."

Holding the envelope up to the light, the technician turned serious. "How old?"

"Three days, maybe four. And it was handled yesterday by a woman named Judith Darr."

"You got her prints?"

Marritt reached into his jacket pocket for a two-by-six-inch fingerprint card. "I took these last night at the precinct house."

"How soon do you need results?"

"Yesterday, if possible."

"That rules out ninhydrin," the technician answered. "Ninhydrin's for slowpokes—forty-eight hours. And dusting don't work so good for prints on paper. What do you say we try iodine fuming?" Still talking, he took a vial of silvery black crystals from a nearby shelf, and sprinkled a gram's worth into the plastic envelope with Klaus Ehrlich's letter. "This stuff works pretty quick. Whenever someone touches something, amino acids get left behind. If we're lucky, the guy who wrote this letter touched his face or hair just before he sent it. That would give us a nice, big, juicy print.''

Portions of Klaus Ehrlich's letter were turning gold. Five, maybe six, prints were emerging.

''That's iodine vapors making the amino acids change color,'' the technician explained. ''Let's visit the camera room and take pictures while the prints are stable.'' Not waiting for a response, he picked up the plastic envelope and crossed to an adjacent room, where a heavy black camera was mounted. Marritt followed.

''If you want to know the truth, this camera stinks. It's twenty years old and lousy as far as contrast photography is concerned. The FBI has a new model—laser photography—but it costs fifty grand, and the City won't blow for one.''

In five minutes, the photographs were complete.

''Let's see what we got,'' Keegan said, holding Judith's fingerprint card up for comparison. ''Prints one and two are tented arches, identical to the thumb of one J. Darr. Three and four match up with her slant loop and whorl. Five is a partial print; in fact, it's useless. That leaves print number six.'' Keegan peered at the photograph, then back at Judith Darr's fingerprint card. ''Print number six don't belong to Judith Darr. If you were smart enough not to touch the letter, print number six is a clue.''

Marritt stood by, digesting the data.

"You got a suspect?" Keegan queried.

"I think so."

"How sure are you it's the right guy?"

Marritt shrugged. "Two years ago, he disappeared after a plane crash. Now it looks like he's back again, but finding him could be a problem."

"You want some friendly advice?"

"Friendly, unfriendly—I'll take any kind."

"Try ninhydrin."

"What would that do?"

"Ninhydrin. This guy who disappeared. Can you get your hands on some letters, papers, something he wrote?"

"I guess so."

"Okay. Get it, and send it to me here at the lab. This ninhydrin is like magic. It's a chemical that turns amino acids purple. You spray it on, wait forty-eight hours, and the prints are there. And the beauty is, it works on amino acids that seeped into paper fibers years ago. That means it gets prints that are thirty, even forty years old."

"You're kidding."

"Richard, I kid you not. Get me an account ledger, a letter, anything this guy had his hands on, and I'll tell you if his prints match up with number six on the letter we got now."

Back at the precinct house, Marritt put in a call for Dema, who was out in the field gathering data. Waiting for his return, the detective drank two cups of coffee and leafed through current case files that needed only his signature to be closed: a local bar accused of serving inferior Scotch from bottles labeled Chivas Regal; a small deli that sold beer on Sunday morning in violation of state blue laws.

Dema arrived just before noon, and Marritt recounted his trip to the lab preparatory to giving instructions: "See what you can do about getting Karl Heiden's personal papers from the Beethoven Museum in Bonn—preferably a diary or ledger that hasn't passed through too many hands."

Then Dema reported on his own endeavors. "I looked into Victor Pesage's past as a conductor. It's there, but it was a long time ago. We might be kidding ourselves in thinking it's relevant."

Marritt waited. The younger cop went on.

"After Pesage failed as a violinist, he tried his hand at conducting. We're talking thirty-five, maybe forty, years ago when he was a student at the Mozarteum in Salzburg. The school's records are incomplete, but it looks as though the faculty jury recommended that he discontinue his conducting studies. One professor dissented, saying Pesage had definite skill and a certain depth of integrity as a conductor, and that the orchestra was at fault for not responding to him properly."

"And?"

"That's it. Pesage dropped out of the Mozarteum, and left Salzburg for Vienna. He spent three decades as a patron of the arts and society figure. Then he began some sort of research project that took him to

Bonn. Given what we know, it's not unreasonable to assume he was working on a study of Beethoven or something along those lines."

"Anything more?"

"I came across some source material that might be helpful—a three-volume collection of Beethoven's letters compiled by a woman named Emily Anderson. They've been translated into English, but there's a German edition if you prefer the original."

"Don't be a wise ass," Marritt grumbled. "How do we get hold of them?"

"There's a copy at the Forty-second Street Public Library."

"How'd you like to read letters tonight?"

"I can't. After work, I've got a martial arts lesson at the Police Academy."

Marritt nodded. "Once upon a time, I knew that stuff. Five, maybe six years ago I took lessons. 'Continuing education' was what they called it."

"Why stop?"

"It took up time I wanted to spend with David and Jonathan. I got lazy. After I made detective, I figured I wouldn't need it. There were a thousand reasons."

"Did you use it?"

"Once. I was on the subway, coming into Manhattan to visit my mother in the hospital. Like a dummy, I didn't have my gun. Those were the days I carried it ninety-nine percent of the time instead of one hundred. Anyway, on the subway this punk pulled out a knife and told me to give him my money. Keep in mind, I wasn't particularly confident about my martial arts ability, but he was standing right in front of me, just right for a karate kick. I figured I could kick him in the knee, which would immobilize him in a hurry, but I might break my toe; or I could kick him in the crotch, which would be better, but it was higher up and I might miss.''

"And?"

"Either way, there was a risk; but the idea of crushing his balls appealed to me, so I went for broke. It was one of the most satisfying moments of my life.''

The telephone rang, interrupting his story, and Marritt picked up the receiver. "I can't," Dema heard him grumble. "I've got to be at the library tonight, reading letters by Beethoven.''

Her recital was only thirteen days off. So much to do, so little time. Yet Judith knew that in some ways those thirteen days could last forever. She was confident about her music. All she needed was to maintain the fine edge she'd already developed, which would be relatively easy, and to coordinate with the pianist chosen to accompany her, which would be marginally harder. She wondered if the accompanist had any idea of the pressure she was under. Probably not. He saw she was nervous, but attributed it to the recital. That was symptomatic of what made her fears so difficult to handle. There wasn't anyone to talk to. Marritt knew the story, and Dema. But she couldn't just pick up the phone and call Marritt each time she wanted reassurance. There had to be a reason for every call—a letter from Ehrlich, a new idea, a clue.

So what could she do? She could practice, polish her recital pieces some more. Tuck the viola under her chin and play Britten and Brahms. But she wasn't in the mood. She was frightened and wanted someone there for security, someone to share the burden. So a little after noon, she decided to call Marritt and invite him over to listen to records. After all, he'd told her he wanted to come back sometime and listen to Beethoven's Ninth.

"I can't," he told her. "I've got to be at the library tonight, reading letters by Beethoven."

But she was pretty insistent, and he sensed her desperation at the other end of the line. So finally, he agreed to come over when he finished reading.

"I'll be there," he promised, "sometime between eight and nine tonight."

Chapter 19

MARRITT HAD TWO REASONS for listening to records
with Judith Darr. First, she was his only link to
solving a triple murder. And second, he still harbored
the notion that understanding Beethoven was part of
the solution. Maybe there was a third, more personal,
reason, but he preferred not to focus on it now.

Judith was wearing jeans and a fitted blouse when
the detective arrived at her apartment. Each time he
saw her, Marritt was more aware of her figure than
he had been the time before.

"I appreciate your coming," she said, welcoming him at the door. "Your being here makes me feel secure." She took his coat. "Would you like some coffee or a glass of wine?"

"Coffee, unless there's a beer in the refrigerator."

There was a bottle of Budweiser. Judith poured it for Marritt, then helped herself to a glass of white wine.

"How were Beethoven's letters?"

"Charming," he answered, "but I was hoping for something more." Following her lead, he settled on the sofa. "At the very least, I'd love to know where Klaus Ehrlich plans on sending you in November. Beethoven lived in Vienna for thirty-five years. It was Pesage's home for almost as long. If November fourth rolls around and you're on a plane to Paris or London—"

His voice trailed off.

It was the first time he'd put into words just how far he expected Judith to go.

"I practiced yesterday," she told him after an awkward pause. "Maybe you'd like to come to my recital. You could bring your family along."

Marritt took a sip of Budweiser. "I'd probably be better off bringing Dema, just in case Ehrlich is around."

There was no answer, and he leaned back on the sofa, wondering what he could say to ease her fears that wouldn't be wrong. "You're pretty disciplined, aren't you?" he finally offered. "What with practice and all."

"I try."

"Is it hard? I mean, suppose my kids wanted to learn to play viola. How long would it take them?"

"That depends. I could show you now."

"Pardon?"

"I could show you. Would you like a lesson?"

Marritt's face reddened.

"Don't be afraid."

"I've never played an instrument before."

"That's all right. Just relax and let me handle the situation." Crossing the room, Judith picked up her viola, brought it back, and handed it to Marritt. "Here. You'll have to stand to do this properly."

The detective rose, cradling the instrument with both hands.

"All right, now the first thing to do is balance the viola on your shoulder so the pressure from your jawbone can hold it steady. Try it—hold the neck of the viola with your left hand."

Carefully, Marritt lodged the chin rest into the space between his shoulder and jaw.

"Good. Now take your hand away and see if the viola balances."

"Why can't I keep holding it with my left hand?"

"Because your hand has to be free to move along the neck of the viola and apply pressure to the strings. Otherwise, you'd only be able to play four notes."

"I can't hold it with just my jaw."

"You have to. And don't drop it. It's worth two hundred thousand dollars."

"How much?"

"Two hundred thousand. It's an Amati, made for the French Royal Court in 1573. I'm poor, but the Rockefeller Foundation has lots of money."

Struggling, the detective managed a precarious balance. "You hold it like this for six hours a day?" he asked incredulously.

"Sure. Now stop complaining while I explain how to stroke the bow. Here, take this in your right hand. Relax; let your fingers fall naturally over the handle."

Marritt felt Judith's hand on top of his own.

"Now bring your thumb around until it meets your middle finger. Balance it by putting your pinky on top of the stick. Good! Now run the bow across the strings between the fingerboard and bridge of the viola. Do it! Come on!"

Slowly, Marritt manipulated the bow. A sort of whining squeal sounded.

"Keep your shoulder down. Don't move your whole arm—just from your wrist to your elbow. Do it again, across all the strings."

The detective repeated his earlier movement.

"Good! That's four notes. A, D, G, and C."

The notes sounded a third time.

"Wonderful! You have a rotten chin, but your bow arm is fantastic."

"What's it made of?" Marritt asked, putting the instrument down.

"Wood—mostly maple and spruce, with a little

ebony. And the bow is pernambuco. It's one of the few woods dense enough to absorb playing pressure when it's cut thin and long. The bow strands are horsehair. Each one has thousands of tiny barbs. The friction of the barbs against the strings is what makes music. The strings are catgut wound around steel."

"What's catgut?"

"Just what it says it is. To make music, you use dead cats and horses. Now would you like to listen to Beethoven?"

Most of what Marritt remembered about Beethoven's Ninth came from his chart: "A mighty hymn of praise and thanksgiving honoring the Brotherhood of Man and Fatherhood of God. Four movements— struggle, humor, contemplation, and jubilation."

Judith put the first record on the turntable and returned to her spot on the sofa beside him. The music began with what sounded like an orchestra tuning up; then there was a series of eerie, hammerlike blows.

Marritt loosened his tie.

"You can take your jacket off," she told him.

He started to, then decided against it, because he was self-conscious about his shoulder holster and gun.

"To understand Beethoven," he heard Judith saying, "you have to compare him with the music that came before—Gregorian chants, Renaissance ballads, the evolution of symphonies through Mozart and Haydn.

No one wrote anything as lush and full and complex as Beethoven. The way he moved energy is almost frightening.''

Marritt listened. The first movement wasn't a melody so much as a conflict between forces. Now and then a soothing force would sweep down, grow, fade, then crescendo.

"I have headphones," Judith offered. "Do you want them?"

"No, thanks. Not being able to hear whatever else was going on would make me nervous. It's my cop training."

The "struggle" lasted for a quarter of an hour. Then the second movement began. Judith sat with her wine glass in one hand and her free arm draped along the back of the sofa, inches from Marritt.

"What do you hear?" she asked the detective.

"A lot of squiggly lines."

Or rather, he *saw* them. The lines grew bolder, darting around, repeating. Little instruments chased one another; then larger instruments followed. They were slipping and sliding and bumping, all falling down.

A new mood began—slow, sweet, thoughtful, contemplative. If anyone had the power to reach across the ages, it was Beethoven. He could stir forces, touch spirits. With simple notes, his music tapped a range of emotions from dissatisfaction and longing to warmth and love. The third movement ended. Now the music was grumbling and low.

"Listen," Judith told him. "The same theme is being played over and over."

The texture was simple and pure, so obvious a melody that any child could master it. The theme grew louder, more bold. Glaciers, waterfalls, all the images Marritt had read about before. He wondered how so simple a melody could contain so much power.

Judith stood up and crossed to her desk, returning with a one-page German-English translation. The Ninth Symphony's chorale finale dawned:

> O friends, no more these sounds!
> Let us sing more cheerful songs, more full of joy!

The voices exulted, ringing on high:

> All creatures drink of joy
> At nature's breast.
>
> Weak and strong
> Alike taste of her gift.

The jubilation crescendoed:

> Thy magic power reunites
> All that custom has divided;
> All men become brothers
> Under the sway of thy gentle wings.

Judith was lost, a faraway look in her eyes:

You millions, I embrace you;
This kiss is for all the world.
Brothers, above the starry canopy
There must dwell a loving Father.
World, do you know your Creator?
Seek him in the Heavens,
Above the stars must He dwell.

Then the music was gone. And silence reigned, until Judith spoke again: "Beethoven was tormented. But he had the greatest reward a composer can know— the recognition of his genius in his own time, the knowledge that he and his music would become immortal."

Marritt sat silent. There was so much he didn't understand about music and art, poetry, drama—and here was Judith Darr, offering him an entrée to it all; giving of herself, sharing as best she knew how.

"They're performing Beethoven's Ninth at Lincoln Center," Judith told him. "We could go together. I mean, it's no big thing. I could get tickets for the week after my recital."

"I'd like that. Really, I would."

Just for a moment, their eyes met. Then Marritt looked down.

"It's late," she said, "and that look says you want to go home. Thank you for being here this evening. Before you came, I was scared and awfully low."

Judith got his coat from the closet and walked him to the door.

"Goodnight."

Then, before they could shake hands, she kissed him. Not a long kiss, but on the lips; gentle and firm.

"I'll see you at the recital," she promised. "If not before."

Chapter 20

"IT'S NOT FAIR," complained David. "He was only closer by one."

"You're being a baby."

"Shut up, Jonathan."

Seven o'clock, the morning after. To the accompanying strains of family discord, Marritt wandered into the kitchen.

"Don't tell me to shut up, David. I'm two years older."

"Double shut up. Shut up twice, Jonathan."

Sitting at the kitchen table, Marritt waited for a break in the action. "What's not fair?" he asked, when able.

"Last night at Cub Scouts," David told him.

"What happened at Cub Scouts?"

"The jelly bean contest." Warming to the presence of a sympathetic listener, David began what was becoming a fairly polished recital. "Last night at Cub Scouts, we had a contest to guess the number of jelly beans in a giant bottle. I guessed three hundred, and Eddie Kanicki guessed three hundred and twenty-seven. The right answer was three hundred and fourteen, so Eddie Kanicki won all the jelly beans."

Marritt waited. The story seemed to be over. "What's the problem?"

"It's not fair. He was only closer by one. How come he gets all the jelly beans, and I get none?"

"Probably because those were the rules of the contest."

"But the rules weren't fair."

The discussion continued, with David grudgingly giving ground on what constituted fairness as opposed to self-interest. When breakfast was over, Marritt walked to the subway station and made his way into Manhattan. First baseman for the New York Yankees; the World Series—his fantasies proliferated as the train rumbled on. More than once, his thoughts drifted to Judith Darr.

Dema was at the precinct house when the detective arrived. He was quieter than usual, almost somber.

"What's the matter?" asked Marritt.

There was a pause—as though the young cop was weighing the wisdom of his answer. . . . "Last night I broke up with my boyfriend. Do you want to hear about it?"

On top of jelly beans and Judith Darr, Marritt needed the specifics of his partner's love life like a hole in the head. "No, Jim, I don't want to hear about you and your boyfriend."

Dema left, after being advised to keep October 18 open for Judith's recital. Marritt leafed through some papers on his desk before turning to a statistical study of crime in New York. According to the Commissioner's office, only two percent of all street muggings resulted in conviction. For apartment burglaries, the figure was even lower. Midway through the study, the detective glanced at a plastic-framed photo of his wife on the shelf to his right. The picture had been taken five years earlier, when she was thirty-seven. Her looks hadn't changed, except now her reddish brown hair was shorter and grayer. And her face, plain-looking and round, was a bit fuller than before. That was all right. Hers wasn't the only face that had grown fuller. Maybe he should go over to the gym and start working out at martial arts with Dema. If nothing else, he'd lose five pounds. Challenge yourself, not your opponent. That was the philosophy of hand-to-hand combat. And he remembered several choke-holds, along with three or four defensive maneuvers, to apply, when unarmed, against an opponent with a knife or gun. But his timing was rusty; the only combat skill that remained was marksmanship. Forget the gym. He was lazy and had too many other things to do.

But let anyone take away his gun, and Marritt knew he'd be in trouble.

The day passed; then two days more. Karl Heiden's diary arrived from the Beethoven Museum in Bonn, and was forwarded to Danny Keegan at the fingerprint laboratory. The *Daily News* published a "retrospective" on "The Murders That Shook New York." Where the police investigation was concerned, the newspaper was far from flattering. Judith didn't call. Marritt bought a Volkswagen for seven thousand dollars. The World Series began. Danny Keegan came to the precinct house in person to report his findings.

"Richard, I checked the diary. I took it apart, sprayed each page, gave it a real going-over. This ninhydrin is incredible."

"I know; you told me."

"Okay, okay. Don't get hostile. Anyway, you know print number six from the letter you brought me—the right slant loop? There's dozens of them smeared all over the diary. It's the same guy."

Dozens of prints—confirmation that Karl Heiden had not died in the plane crash, that he was still alive. The Beethoven theory was viable.

Back to the library; more research on Beethoven. Marritt's note cards mounted: Through much of his life, Beethoven suffered from syphilis, the scourge of his era. His terminal symptoms corresponded with hepatitis and cirrhosis of the liver. He was born a

Catholic, but never practiced as one; there was no record of his having attended mass or gone to confession. He detested teaching; his spelling was atrocious. Mathematics had been a source of impenetrable mystery to him.

But nothing on a Tenth Symphony.

The days went by. Judith's recital drew closer. Several times, Marritt pondered whether or not Klaus Ehrlich would attend. Probably not; but if he did, what then? What could Marritt do—arrest him? On what charge—giving away tens of thousands of dollars, or being an accessory to murder, when there was nothing more than circumstantial evidence that the victims had even spoken with him?

The weekend was followed by more work in the library. Beethoven, according to one commentator, relied heavily on classical literature for inspiration and peace of mind. References to Shakespeare, Plutarch, and Homer appeared frequently in his writings. Several months before the composer died, he turned in desperation to a new remedy for deafness—green nut rinds crushed in lukewarm milk, a drop in each ear every few hours. Of his mother, Beethoven wrote, "She was such a good, kind mother, and indeed my very best friend. Oh, who was happier than I, when I could still utter the sweet name of mother and it was heard and answered."

More notes, mostly quotes from books that Marritt was reading: "There will never be a time when Beethoven's work is not central to the musical mind. . . ." "Beethoven took music beyond the pleasure principle of Viennese classicism. He permitted aggressive and disintegrative forces to enter musical form. . . .'' ''If we lose our awareness of the transcendent realms of beauty and brotherhood portrayed in the great affirmative works of our culture, if we lose the dream of the Ninth Symphony, there will remain no counterpoise against the engulfing tremors of civilization, nothing to set against Auschwitz and Vietnam as paradigms of the human mind.''

But nothing on Symphony Number Ten.

The World Series ended. Marritt began getting addicted to old ''Honeymooners'' reruns on television. David got 103 on his first math exam of the school year.

''How can you get over one hundred?'' Marritt wondered.

''There was an extra-credit question,'' David told him.

There was no word from Judith Darr. Marritt thought of telephoning to find out if she was all right. She was probably just busy preparing for her recital; better to leave well enough alone. After the recital, he could give her a call. Still, he missed her. He'd never felt that way about a witness before, and he wasn't sure it was a good idea to feel that way about one now.

October 16. October 17. On the morning of the 18th, as Marritt entered the precinct house, the desk sc̤geant flagged him down.

''Richard, you got a package upstairs on your desk. I think it's a bomb.'' Before Marritt could answer, the desk sergeant added: "Just joking. Actually, a real sweet-looking gal brought it by. I checked her for identification, just to make sure."

More anxious than he realized, Marritt climbed the stairs to the second floor. On the center of his desk was a gift-wrapped box, maybe an inch deep and thirteen inches square. A plain white envelope, marked "Lieutenant Richard Marritt," was taped to the outside.

Marritt opened the envelope and read the note, written in a clear, legible hand:

Dear Richard,

I'm not quite sure how to say this, but I want to thank you for being who you are. These past eight weeks have been terrifying for me in ways I'll never be able to describe. The only thing that's kept me sane is the knowledge that you're there. I don't expect miracles. I know there are things you can't control. But I want you to know how grateful I am that you're on my side, and that you care.

I've left recital tickets for you and Officer Dema at the New School box office. The recital starts at eight o'clock tonight. Also, if you're still interested, there's a performance of Beethoven's Ninth next Thursday at Lincoln Center.

Thank you again.

Judith Darr

Marritt unwrapped the box. Inside was a set of records: *The Complete Symphonic Works of Ludwig van Beethoven.*

The New School auditorium was located on 12th Street between Fifth and Sixth avenues. Marritt and Dema arrived for Judith's recital at seven-thirty, picked up their tickets at the box office, and went inside. The stage was bare, except for a black music stand and grand piano. All seats were unreserved.

The two cops stood at the rear of the auditorium and watched the audience file in. The size of the crowd surprised them. By seven forty-five, virtually all five hundred seats had been taken. Anxious to avoid being part of a standing-room-only group, Marritt sat down and Dema followed. A good percentage of the audience was elderly. Marritt recognized some of the younger members as ones he had interviewed. There was no sign of Klaus Ehrlich.

Just before eight o'clock, the detective glanced at the mimeographed program that had been handed to him at the door:

JUDITH DARR, Viola

BACH: Suite in G Major
Prelude
Allemande
Courante
Sarabande
Minuet
Gigue

REGER: Suite No. 1
Molto sostenuto
Vivace
Andante sostenuto
Molto vivace

Intermission

BRITTEN: "Lachrymae," Op. 48

BRAHMS: Sonata in E Flat Major
Allegro amabile
Allegro appassionato
Andante con moto

Piano accompaniment by Nicholas Weissman

The lights dimmed. Judith walked on stage and the audience applauded. Marritt stared. He was looking at a different woman. The T-shirts and jeans and piled-up hair he knew her by were gone. In their stead, she was wearing a long, lilac-colored gown. Her hair was pulled back, held in place by a silver clip that allowed it to flow in a gentle stream well past her shoulders. She looked extraordinarily elegant and warm.

The applause subsided, and Judith smiled. Then the first notes from her viola sounded, rich and full. Her face was relaxed. The audience was charmed. Her listeners were no longer a threat, if ever they had been one. They were a stimulus, an incentive for Judith to reach for a higher goal. All the months of preparation and work had been worthwhile.

Judith Darr was in total command.

Marritt watched the emotions on her face, her intensity and excitement, her longing and devotion. He knew now what an incredibly important moment this was for her; how long she'd worked toward a single goal; the pressure she'd endured; what this night meant to her. And he felt a range of emotions of his own, things he hadn't experienced in a long time. He was moved by Judith Darr. He was proud of her. And then it occurred to him that the last thing in the world he wanted to happen might be happening. For reasons he didn't understand, he felt he might be falling in love with Judith Darr.

Chapter 21

HE HAD CONSIDERED SENDING ROSES. After all, the recital was a major occasion, calling for proper observance by all of goodwill. But then other matters intervened. Pesage had summoned him back to Europe, and he'd been too busy dealing with substantive issues to worry about flowers. Now those other tasks had been completed. All that remained was the nagging problem of the police detective and Judith Darr. He had watched them for some time. Marritt, in particular, was a source of fascination—an obviously uneducated man, but remarkable for his perseverance and driving determination. It was difficult to evaluate precisely how much he and Miss Darr knew; but then they too were ignorant regarding the extent of his own knowledge.

The question, then, was one of timing. If the detective and Judith Darr were disposed of now, the New York authorities would assume further killings were possible, if not planned. In such an event, and with their only link to the murders gone, the police would be quite vocal in warning others of the dangers involved. That would mean an end to the project. And so, for the moment, it was best to lead Marritt and his musician friend on. They could be eliminated at a more suitable hour, closer to fulfillment of the plan.

Chapter 22

Watching Judith Darr perform, something had happened to Marritt. He'd felt it before, listening to records and talking about Beethoven; but it hadn't been this strong. Now he was captivated and more than a little confused by the effect of it all.

He called to congratulate her the day after the recital. Her telephone was busy for a long time. When he finally got through, she was exuberant and warm. "It went really well," she told him. "With luck, it will open quite a few doors." He thanked her for the records. She asked if he still wanted to hear Beethoven's Ninth at Lincoln Center. They agreed to meet Thursday night at Avery Fisher Hall.

The days passed. Marritt's wife caught a cold. Jonathan quit Little League Football because "the coach is a moron." Marritt concurred. "You don't need uniforms; you don't need coaches," he told Dema the following afternoon. "Just let the kids play."

The rest of the week, the detective spent a fair amount of time sitting at his desk, thinking about Judith Darr. What struck him most was how his mental picture of her had evolved. At their first meeting, he had noticed her eyes and her smile. Her face had seemed plain, almost ordinary, that afternoon. Later, he'd become more aware of her body—full breasts, narrow hips, legs that would do a dancer proud. And all the while, her face was becoming more familiar, easier to look at—until recital night when he had seen the beauty behind it all.

They met Thursday night for Beethoven's Ninth at Lincoln Center in the lobby of Avery Fisher Hall. Judith was wearing a straight skirt and blue silk blouse. Most everyone in the lobby was dressed in expensive suits and lavish gowns. Judith took two tickets from her purse as they approached the door.

"How much were they?" Marritt asked.

"Don't worry about it. Think of it as coming out of Klaus Ehrlich's ten thousand dollars."

The concert hall was beige, gold, cream-colored and brown—unlike any hall the detective had seen before. An usher showed them to their seats. Marritt told Judith he'd listened to Beethoven's Ninth on the records she'd given him the week before. "I didn't find any clues, but it will help me enjoy the music more."

Judith was quieter than usual. "When in the presence of Beethoven's Ninth," she explained, "I'm pretty humble."

At eight o'clock, the orchestra appeared on stage. Most of its members were older than the freelancers Marritt had interviewed. He felt awkward, a little out of place in the concert hall. "Relax," Judith whispered, touching his hand. "Just enjoy the music."

He wondered what his wife was thinking; what she'd felt when he'd told her he was going to Lincoln Center "with a witness named Judith Darr."

The music began.

Marritt thought back to things he'd read and learned mere weeks before: "Beethoven's music defines the purpose of an orchestra. From simple notes on sheets of paper, he created mighty cathedrals to the Gods. . . . No moment in a symphony, however beautiful, is as important as its place within the whole. The tip of a peak in a range of mountains is special because of its surroundings. . . . Beethoven is immortal; he stands above time, alone."

At the symphony's end, the silence of the audience gave way to loud, sustained applause. Marritt sat in his chair, appreciating what he'd heard, but feeling a little left out and alone. He sensed a gulf between the knowledge possessed by those around him and his own. These people had grown up listening to Beethoven. They understood Mozart, Haydn, and Brahms. He was an intruder, who didn't really understand at all.

"It's over," Judith told him. "Will you buy me something to eat before we go home?"

They walked to a cafe near Lincoln Center, one of many that had grown in popularity during the revitalization of Manhattan's Upper West Side. A waitress about Judith's age led them to a window table. Marritt read the menu: quiche, mushrooms, a lot of salads; heavy on fish, only a few meat entrées.

"What's a sorbet?" he asked.

"It's like sherbet," Judith answered.

"What's the difference?"

"I don't know."

They ordered drinks. The tables were arranged in a manner that suggested intimacy. The waitress returned, put their drinks on the table, and asked if they knew what they wanted for dinner. Judith ordered a spinach salad; Marritt, the hamburger platter.

"Red meat isn't good for you," Judith cautioned.

The detective gave her a sideways look.

"I think what we have here is a clash of cultures," she told him. "Eat your hamburger."

The cafe was crowded for a Thursday night. Judith alternated between playing with her swizzle stick and sipping her drink. "It's strange," she said, looking toward Marritt. "Ever since we met, you've been asking questions about me. I haven't asked about you at all.''

''What would you like to know?''

''Whatever you think is important. What sort of music you like; how long you've been a detective; what it's like to be a cop.''

The salad and hamburger platter arrived together. Marritt ordered another drink. ''I joined the force nineteen and a half years ago. I was in uniform for eight years; then they made me a detective up in Harlem. Seven years ago, I got transferred to the West Side. In eight months, I'm eligible to retire on three-quarters pension. Maybe I'll stay on; maybe I'll look around for another job. There's not much opportunity out there for ex-cops.''

''Did you ever want to be anything else?''

''Not really. I fantasize a lot, but I'm a cop.''

''What do you fantasize about?''

Marritt adjusted the silverware on the table. ''It's silly. I mean, it's only a fantasy—sometimes on the subway, to make things go faster, I pretend I'm a major league baseball player. I mean, I'm forty-four years old. There's no way it could happen, but I think about it.''

The waitress returned with a bottle of catsup for Marritt. Judith poured some vinaigrette dressing on her spinach salad. ''I fantasize too; everyone does.''

''What do you fantasize about?''

''Solo performances with the world's great orchestras. Triumphant tours of Europe and Asia. There's no harm in daydreaming as long as you separate fantasy from reality.''

''Do you?''

''Most of the time.''

They talked for an hour. Afterward, Marritt paid the check, and they began to walk toward Judith's apartment. Broadway was slowing down for the night. In the eighties, they turned onto West End Avenue.

''Are you happy?'' asked Judith.

The question caught Marritt off-guard.

''Sure. I mean, I've got headaches like everyone else. But life at home is pretty good. My wife and I have two wonderful children. The guys I work with are my friends. Put it together, and I got nothing to complain about. What about you? Are you happy?''

''I don't know. Sometimes I think maybe I'm too involved with my music, that I use it as an excuse to shut people out. All my life, I've been into getting rid of beliefs rather than having them. Now I'm not sure what to think.''

They drew closer to Judith's apartment, their hands brushing together from time to time. Maybe the touching was by accident. Marritt wasn't sure. But, unless his imagination was playing tricks on him, there was a definite physical tension between them.

''I like you, you know that,'' he heard Judith saying. ''But in some ways you seem like an old forty-four.''

''What are you—my psychiatrist?''

''I'm your friend. I feel close to you. But sometimes you're very standoffish.''

Time was running out. What he really wanted was to hold her. Maybe she wanted to have an affair with him. That was the reason for the things she was saying. He had to get straight in his mind the difference between love and fascination, between what was right and what was wrong.

If she invites me upstairs, Marritt wondered, should I go? It was too confusing. All he knew was what he wanted—and maybe what was best. Just once, he told himself. Just once, and maybe it would get Judith Darr out of his system. If not—

They came to the stoop of her apartment building on 87th Street.

Marritt had made up his mind.

Judith looked at her watch. "Would you like to come upstairs for something to drink?"

"All right."

A little nervous, he followed her through the front door into the vestibule.

"I was out all day. Let me check the mailbox first."

There didn't seem to be much—a form letter soliciting funds from the American Cancer Society, a brochure from Sears-Roebuck. And one letter, enclosed in a plain white envelope. Judith opened it, and Marritt knew from the look on her face that there'd be no affair that night:

Dear Miss Darr,

  Enclosed are tickets for your journey, which begins on November 4th. Upon arriving at Wien Airport, please proceed by taxi to the Intercontinental Hotel at 1 Johannesgasse 28. Accommodations have been reserved in your name. You must bring with you a black evening gown, your passport, your viola, and, of course, the music.

Kindest regards,
Klaus Ehrlich

Judith stared at the letter and the tickets. Her hands trembled; her face was white. It was happening—the next act in this insane, bizarre, deadly plot.

"Where?" asked Marritt.

"It's Vienna."

Chapter 23

MARRITT'S JOB WAS IN NEW YORK CITY. He'd never traveled outside the United States, and nothing in the police union contract required him to. Still, this was his case, and the solution lay four thousand miles away in Europe. That was one rationale for going to Vienna. The other was Judith Darr. He'd never forgive himself if anything happened to her. What he needed, then, was to square his conscience with leaving his wife and children behind, and the only way to do that was by being professional. He'd go to Vienna but, insofar as possible, he'd treat Judith like any other witness. That meant the affair between them would have to be over before it had begun.

The days that followed seemed to blur. There was so much to do and so little time. Get a passport. Explain to David and Jonathan where he was going. Consult with the Commissioner's office. Analyze new clues. He and Judith talked by telephone several times.

"I'm sort of excited," she told him. "I mean, I'm scared but I'm excited too. I keep thinking about the Ringstrasse and Sacher tortes and museums—and the music."

Marritt and Dema went through the case file, clue by clue. There wasn't much that was new, other than a photograph of Victor Pesage forwarded by Interpol. Marritt studied the portrait and focused on the eyes. They were intense, burning.

Judith's plane ticket had been issued in Vienna by Royal Jordanian Airlines. The company's records showed an over-the-counter cash transaction. "I booked you on the same flight," Dema reported. "Leaving New York at nine-forty the night of November fourth, coming back the afternoon of November ninth."

"In other words, I'm being flown to Vienna by a bunch of Arabs."

The young cop shrugged, then went on. "The Commissioner's office asked Interpol to run a check of concert halls in Vienna to see what performances are being planned. Every auditorium reservation they found corresponds with a known orchestra. The only

other thing I could think of to do was reserve a room
for you at the Intercontinental Hotel, where Judith is
staying. Actually, this could turn out to be a fairly
nice junket.''

"Tell that to my wife. She's scared stiff I'm coming back in a coffin.''

Dema didn't answer.

"By the way,'' Marritt asked, continuing the conversation. "Where is Vienna? I mean, I know it's in
Austria, but what part of the country?''

"I'm not sure. I think it's forty or fifty miles from
the Czechoslovakian border.''

The detective's eyes widened. "But the Austrians
are on our side, right? What I mean is, on top of
everything else, if the Communists are mixed up in
this, I'm staying home.''

Reviewing the case file took the better part of the
afternoon. Midway through his third cup of coffee,
Marritt thought to ask what language they spoke in
Vienna, and learned to his dismay that the answer
was German. "I talked to the Austrian version of the
FBI,'' Dema added, pointing the way toward solution of the problem. "They promised that someone
who speaks English will be available if needed.''

"Anything else?''

"Just be careful. A live cop is better than a dead
one.''

It was all happening quickly, too quickly in fact
for Marritt to feel comfortable. Ten weeks earlier
there hadn't even been a murder. Then there were
three bodies, and after that, the hint of a plan. But

even as things crystallized, he really hadn't had time to adjust to the notion of going abroad. Now events were catching up with him. Maybe it was the anxiety of a trip away from home, of leaving his wife for the first time. Maybe it was that he didn't know what would happen when he got to Vienna. Maybe it was fear, a fear long realized, that he was facing a machine far more deadly and methodical than the ordinary street criminals he had known. Whatever the reason, the fear was growing and on departure day, November 4, Richard Marritt began to reflect on the fact that he was mortal.

Travel alarm clock, pajamas, underwear, socks . . . as Marritt moved around the house packing his belongings, the fear reached new proportions. Passport, plane tickets, shirts, back-up tie . . . He wondered why he was going. Was it really necessary? Would he still be going if his link to the crime had been someone other than Judith Darr? Toothbrush, electric shaver, deodorant, dental floss . . . Three people had been murdered, maybe four. Tens of thousands of dollars had been put into the enemy plan. Who was he kidding? There was no way he could measure up to that kind of opposition. He would call it off— phone Judith Darr, tell her it was over and stay home. But the whole thing had taken on an impetus of its own. He was going to Vienna.

The trip to Kennedy Airport took a little more than an hour in evening traffic. Marritt drove; his wife sat beside him. David and Jonathan were in the backseat of the Volkswagen. Queens Boulevard. The Van Wyck

Expressway. The detective's thoughts wandered. For twelve years he and his wife had been married. For twelve years his wife had wanted to go to Europe, and there'd always been an excuse for not going. Don't think about it, he decided. Think about television or playing ball.

The sky was overcast, not a particularly good omen. Marritt drove past the airport parking lot to the International Departures Terminal. "Remember," he told David and Jonathan, "be good while I'm gone. And do what your mother tells you to do." He kissed them good-bye, and then he was alone, standing on the curb outside the terminal building. He wondered if anyone inside was watching. Probably not, but as a precaution he and Judith had agreed to sit in different rows on the plane. At the check-in counter, he traded his suitcase for an aisle-seat assignment in the no-smoking section. "The plane leaves at nine-forty," the woman behind the counter told him. "Boarding is at nine o'clock at gate number five."

With thirty minutes to spare, Marritt went to the boarding area, and flashed his badge to get his police revolver through the security checkpoint. Judith was already there, sitting by the far wall, her viola beside her. They acknowledged each other with their eyes. There was no sign of Klaus Ehrlich. A little after nine, boarding began. Judith picked up her viola and carried it onto the plane. Marritt followed to a seat five rows behind her.

Nine-fifteen. Nine-twenty. A young man about thirty came into the cabin, carrying a case the size of a

violin. The detective watched him move down the
aisle toward a seat in the rear. The air was stuffy.
Marritt stood up, took off his jacket, and wedged it
into the compartment above. The aircraft took off.
He looked down at the New York City lights disappearing below, then moved his watch ahead by
six hours. In Vienna, it was three forty-five in the
morning.

Dinner was prototype airline food: baked chicken,
peas, mashed potatoes, lettuce with a cherry tomato,
a hard roll, butter, some sort of strawberry pudding.
Marritt picked at his food. After the stewardess had
taken his tray away, he went to the lavatory to brush
his teeth; then leaned back and closed his eyes.

Judith sat on the plane, unable to sleep as people
dozed around her. So much was happening, so much
was going through her mind. Why was she here?
Why had she put herself in this position? What if she
had simply stood up moments before takeoff and
walked off the plane? The day after her recital, why
couldn't she have fallen and broken her arm? Then
she wouldn't have been able to play the viola, and
Ehrlich or Heiden or whatever his name was, whoever was watching, would have known she couldn't
play, and left her alone.

Thank God for Marritt! At least there was someone
to protect her—her own private policeman, and more.
He understood her fear and dread of the unknown.

And he shared her hope that the killing was over, that Pesage or Heiden or whoever was in charge would have her perform and then let her go home.

Maybe something good would come of it all. Maybe something momentous in the world of music was going on, and because of what was happening she would be privy to it all. Maybe she would get to hear Heiden's music as a whole. Viewed in that light, the prospects weren't uniformly awful. And there was one other possible benefit, strange but real. Judith's life as a musician involved more than playing. It was built on knowledge and an appreciation of music—its history, its components, the ways it could be taken apart and fitted together again. In all her life, no one she had known had revealed a greater command of that realm than Klaus Ehrlich. As scared as she was, Judith wanted the experience of listening to Ehrlich talk about music again.

Marritt couldn't sleep. He had drifted off for maybe an hour, but that was all. The cabin was stuffier than before. He wished he were home. He would pass the time by daydreaming until the plane landed. The baseball fantasy wasn't working, not even when he re-created the World Series in his mind. All he wanted was to be back in Queens with his family, safe and sound.

The sky outside the aircraft brightened. Breakfast was served—orange sections, coffee, and a croissant with butter and strawberry jam. Several rows ahead, Judith was talking with the woman beside her. Finishing breakfast, Marritt went to the lavatory to wash his face and hands.

The plane landed in Vienna on time—11:30 A.M.; 5:30 A.M. New York time. Don't think like that, Marritt told himself. It will blow your mind. The passengers disembarked. Bleary-eyed, unshaven, he followed the others to an area marked Passport Control. Once through customs, signs in German and English led him to the baggage-claim area. Marritt and Judith stood on opposite sides of the carousel as suitcases came tumbling down. Playing a hunch, the detective gravitated toward the young man who had come on the plane carrying a violin.

"Excuse me. Would you like to share a taxi into town? I'm going to the Intercontinental."

"Sorry," the man answered. "I'm staying at the Hilton."

Strike one for intuition, Marritt thought. Anyway, he'd tried. There was probably no connection at all.

Judith's suitcase came off the feeder. She took it, gave Marritt an over-the-shoulder glance, and walked out the door. Several more suitcases passed down, then a woman carrying a large case shaped like a cello walked into the baggage area. She reached onto the carousel for a suitcase with a sticker that indicated it had been shipped from Chicago, turned, and walked away. One plane, three musicians.

At last, the detective's luggage was coming down. Maybe he should wait to see if any instruments came out of the baggage hold. Ten minutes passed. The last passengers picked up their luggage. There had been Judith, one cellist, and the violinist, plus whatever instruments he hadn't seen that had fit into suitcases.

Outside, the November air was fresh and cold. Marritt took several deep breaths, and walked toward a row of taxis parked at the curb. Dema had given him $50.00 in schillings, more than enough to tide him over until he reached the Intercontinental Hotel. The taxi meter showed 22 schillings when the ride began. At six cents a schilling, that was a little more than a $1.30. The ride took thirty minutes; total cost, $17.00 American. At the hotel desk, Marritt checked into room 524. Not bad; actually, it was very nice by the detective's standards. A little small, but what could he expect. The Commissioner's office had approved the Intercontinental, but instructed Dema to reserve the cheapest room possible.

Judith walked into her room and stared. It wasn't a room—it was an honest-to-goodness *suite*, the first she'd ever seen. There was a bedroom, living room, dressing area, and two baths—all hers. Absolutely gorgeous. Moving back and forth between the rooms, she took inventory. The richly carpeted living room was huge, with a desk, coffee table, sofa, two end tables, breakfront, chairs, and a twenty-one-inch color television. The bedroom was almost as large, with two beds, an antique dresser, bureau, more chairs,

220 **Thomas Hauser**

and another television. A bucket of champagne, icy cold, stood on a small table near the door. The elegant dressing area had a makeup table with a three-way mirror framed by light bulbs on the top and sides.

The telephone rang. She picked up the receiver.

"Anything new?" Marritt asked her.

"Richard, you have to see where I am. It's incredible!"

"Later, after I take a nap."

"But we're in Vienna. How can you sleep?"

"I'm tired, and forty-four years old."

At Marritt's suggestion, they made plans to meet for dinner at six-thirty in the hotel lobby. "My intuition tells me it's safe," he told her. "Meanwhile, I'm in room five twenty-four if you need anything. Be careful."

Hanging up the telephone, Judith went back to exploring. The bathroom was The Yellow Room, she decided. Plush yellow towels, yellow bathmat, a fully mirrored wall that reflected all the yellow. In the wardrobe closet, there was a yellow terry-cloth robe. On a marble shelf by the tub, a yellow rose and fern stood in a crystal vase, a small vial of bath oil nearby. Judith turned on the water, poured some oil into the bath, and shed the clothes she'd worn for too many hours. It was two o'clock; she had four hours until she and Marritt would meet for dinner.

For the next hour, Judith luxuriated in the bath, sipping champagne, glancing occasionally at the rose, and thinking how wonderful it would be if all she had to do was hang around the Intercontinental Hotel for five days, play a concert, and then go home. Somehow though, that didn't seem likely. So around three o'clock, determined to take advantage of the situation while it lasted, she got out of the tub, dressed, and went out to see the sights of Vienna.

Chapter 24

THE CHAMPS ÉLYSÉES IN PARIS, the Via del Corso in Rome.

There are a handful of truly great thoroughfares known throughout the world. In Vienna, there is the Ringstrasse.

Two blocks west of the Intercontinental Hotel, Judith came to the Ring. The sun was shining; for November, it was warm. Traveling in a clockwise rotation, she made her way around what had once been the perimeter of old Vienna. The Staat Opera

and Hofburg Palace; ornate buildings; imperial grandeur on either side. It was easy to understand how
Mozart, Beethoven, Strauss, and Brahms had been
inspired in these surroundings. Off to the right, the
gothic spire of St. Stephen's Cathedral pierced the
sky. There were the Museum of Fine Arts, Austria's
Parliament Building, and more churches and statues
than Judith could count.

Once or twice she looked around to see if she was
being followed, but saw no one who looked suspicious. Maybe Klaus Ehrlich would make good on his
promise that nothing improper would be asked of her
or involved. She wondered what Beethoven would
think of it all.

She walked for three hours, until darkness fell and
she went back to the hotel to freshen up for dinner.
The walk had made her feel good. For whatever
reason, she had the distinct feeling that Beethoven
was on her side.

Marritt slept until five in the afternoon. Then the
travel alarm clock sounded and woke him from a
deep slumber. He shaved, showered, put on a clean
shirt, and went downstairs to meet Judith for dinner.

It was only six o'clock, a half hour early. With
time to spare, he crossed the lobby to the hotel gift
shop and thumbed through the postcards, looking for
something appropriate to send David and Jonathan.
Like most of the hotel staff, the woman behind the
counter spoke English, but with a heavy German

accent. Marritt paid for the cards and counted his change, which, for all he knew, could have been Monopoly money. At the main desk, he bought some stamps and exchanged a hundred dollars' worth of traveler's checks for schillings.

Judith met him in the lobby a little after six-thirty. The hotel had two dining rooms—one a standard coffee shop, the other, a more elaborate restaurant called The Rotisserie. At her urging ("Remember, I have ten thousand dollars!") they chose the latter, and were the first couple seated inside.

The restaurant had a low-keyed elegance that Marritt found pleasant and unintimidating. An ice-sculpture of an eagle overlooked the dessert tray nearby. Soft piano music filtered through the air. They ordered drinks, and Marritt looked at the table setting in front of him—four forks, four knives, two spoons. He wasn't sure what to do with all the silverware. Several other couples entered and were seated at various points around the room. With help from the waiter, he and Judith ordered a smoked-fish appetizer for two and a carafe of house wine. Then the main course: red snapper for Judith, roast beef for Marritt.

"It was pretty out there," Judith said, recounting her walk. "All my life, I've wanted to see Vienna. There was a moment this afternoon when I saw the sun reflecting off the Imperial Palace and, in spite of everything, I felt very lucky to be here."

The waiter returned and took away two of Marritt's forks and knives. The wine was poured. Judith began to sip it slowly and looked toward her dinner partner.

"How long do you think it will be before I hear from Ehrlich?"

"I don't know; probably not much longer." Marritt reached for a roll, broke it open, and covered the open face with butter. "My guess is, Klaus Ehrlich has musicians gathering all over Vienna. Most likely, he's just waiting for everyone to arrive."

The appetizers were good. Dinner came with the house salad. Marritt ordered another carafe of wine. He began to let his defenses down, loosen up a little. "You know something?" he wanted to tell her. "If I have to be stuck in Vienna, risking my life for someone, I'm glad it's you. I like you; you're my friend." He wanted to tell her, but he didn't. Somehow, it didn't seem right. So, instead, he made small talk until he found himself saying, "You know what the trouble is with you young people today? You don't form any lasting attachments. You live alone; you never get married. Whatever happened to personal commitment?"

Judith sipped at her wine, digesting his comments. "What about you? You were thirty-two when you and your wife got married. That gives me six years to find a partner."

She was a little tipsy from the wine; they both were.

"Richard, did you love your wife when the two of you got married?"

"Of course I loved her."

"But did you really? What I mean is, when you talk about her, it's always 'my wife this' and 'my wife that.' Sometimes it's as though she doesn't even have a name. And it confuses the hell out of me because my life is complicated and I don't have all the answers. Did you love her when you got married? Do you love her now?''

Marritt sat still, not sure what to say. Finally he came up with: "Judith, I can't give you any easy answers."

"Fine—except that's not good enough for me now. Because too often I'm lonely. I've slept with people who didn't mean a thing to me, and let people I might have cared about drift from my life without ever touching hands. I don't know if I'm asking too much of myself or giving too little to other people, or if there's anything besides music that I know or understand."

The depth of her feelings and the way she expressed them caught Marritt by surprise. He started to answer, but the waiter approached and started clearing away the dishes. And, by the time he was done, Judith was bringing the conversation to a close.

"I'm sorry. I didn't mean to lay my personal problems on you. You've got enough trouble dealing with my other ones. I've had too much to drink, and I'm suffering from jet lag. I'm scared half to death, and I haven't slept for thirty hours. Maybe the thing to do is call it a night. I'll be better company for you in the morning."

They left the restaurant, and took the elevator to Judith's suite on the ninth floor. At the door, Marritt kissed her good night, then went back to his room

and wrote out postcards to his wife and children.
Nine hours later, after a sound sleep, he awoke,
shaved, showered, and dialed Judith's room number.

"I'm sleeping," she announced. "Call me back
when my hangover's gone."

Hungry, the detective went downstairs to the coffee shop for breakfast. Across the room, a young
Japanese man sat alone at a table. The underside of
his jaw was marked by the same type of discoloration
Marritt had seen while interviewing dozens of string
players during the summer.

What day was it! November 6. Judith's return
flight to New York was scheduled for November 9.
He should probably contact the local authorities now,
so that he could call on them quickly, if necessary.
Dema had written out a name and telephone number—
Inspector Friedrich Edmaier, 54–3001. Back in his
room, Marritt dialed the number and, after some
difficulty, was put through to Edmaier by a German-
speaking police operator. When their conversation
was finished, the detective telephoned Judith a second time. "Edmaier and I are meeting in the hotel
lobby at ten-thirty," he reported. "I'll call you when
the meeting's over."

Edmaier turned out to be a large, friendly man
with thinning hair. He was five, maybe ten, years
older than Marritt, and carried himself with an aura
of lethargy. They met as planned and, at the Austri-

an's suggestion, walked outside across the street to Stadt Park.

"Herr Marritt, I trust you've had no troubles here in Vienna?"

"So far everything has been fine."

"And without a doubt, it will remain so. Our city really is quite free from trouble." They walked through the park toward a grove of poplar trees. "Most tourists have no need to call upon our services," the inspector continued. "But of course it is a pleasure to make a courtesy call such as this upon a visiting American police official." He paused, trying to reconcile courtesy with candor. "Herr Marritt, if I may speak frankly, I have been advised of the brutal murders in your country, and also of your opinion regarding the existence of a Tenth Symphony by Beethoven. With all due respect, I must voice my opinion that you Americans are a violent and extremely imaginative people."

There it was! Short of a dead body in the heart of Vienna, there would be no help from Friedrich Edmaier. His words and tone made it clear that he didn't take Marritt seriously. They walked for about an hour, but their conversation was all pro forma. Then Marritt returned to the Intercontinental Hotel and went upstairs to telephone Judith. There was no answer. She was probably eating breakfast, or in the shower. Marritt went downstairs to the hotel coffee shop. She wasn't there. Again, he telephoned her room—still nothing. A current of fear rippled through him. Don't panic! he told himself. She must be in the

shower. Go to her room and listen through the door
for the sound of running water.

The elevator seemed to take forever. On the ninth
floor he walked down the corridor. The door to
Judith's suite was wide open. Inside, a maid was
vacuuming. Marritt approached her.

The maid looked up, switched off the vacuum, and
said something in German.

From where he was standing Marritt could see into
the bedroom. Both beds were made, none of Judith's
belongings were in sight—no clothes, no suitcase.

"Where is she? What happened to the woman who
was here?"

"Wer denken sie; sind dass sie sich so benehmen."

What was she saying? Why didn't the Viennese
speak English? Shouldering his way past the maid,
Marritt picked up the telephone and dialed the hotel
operator.

"Hello! I'd like to know where I can find Miss
Judith Darr. She's a guest in the hotel. . . . Room
901. We arrived here together yesterday. . . . Please!
It's urgent."

Twenty seconds. Thirty. Finally the hotel operator
came back on the line.

"I'm sorry, sir. Fräulein Darr checked out of the
hotel this morning."

Chapter 25

IT HAD HAPPENED QUICKLY, with surgical precision. The telephone rang and then a voice had said: "Miss Darr; this is Klaus Ehrlich. It is imperative that you bring your belongings to the lobby immediately."

"But—"

"There is no time for discussion. You must be downstairs within ten minutes."

The line went dead.

What to do? Judith tried not to panic. She called Marritt but there was no answer. It took her ten minutes to get dressed and stuff her clothes into her suitcase. She'd have to leave a note for the detective downstairs at the checkout desk.

Frantically, Judith grabbed a pencil. "Richard Marritt, Room 524," she scrawled on a piece of hotel stationery. Then she folded the paper over and wrote: "Ehrlich came. He gave me ten minutes. Will call when able."

Cramming the note into her pocket, she reached for her suitcase and viola, left the room, and took the elevator to the lobby floor.

"Miss Darr?"

Judith turned. A man of about forty came toward her. "This way, please."

"But I have to check out."

"Your hotel bill has been taken care of."

"But—"

"We must hurry. There is no time to waste."

He led her through the lobby and outside to the hotel driveway, where a taxi stood with the motor idling. There was no sign of Ehrlich. The back door of the cab was open. The man gestured for Judith to get in, then slid in beside her, while the driver put her suitcase and viola in the trunk.

"Where are we going?"

There was no answer. The car pulled away from the curb. Judith watched as the street signs passed by. *Landstrasse. Erdbergstrasse.* Several miles later they came to a halt near a vacant lot.

"Come with me, please."

Nervously, Judith climbed out of the taxi. The lot

was overgrown with weeds and strewn with abandoned construction material. Despite being in the midst of an urban center, it was every bit as isolated as the narrow corridor that stretched between the Metropolitan Opera House and Damrosch Park at Lincoln Center. Across the lot, Judith could see a bus waiting. She and her escort approached it, and he motioned for her to step on board.

There were fifteen rows of seats with an aisle up the middle; room for sixty passengers. Most of the seats were filled with young men and women. No one was talking. A young man of about thirty gestured to an empty seat beside him. Silently, Judith accepted the offer. She waited, confused, shaken, still not talking. Several more people boarded. Then a black limousine pulled up, and out stepped Ehrlich/Heiden/or whatever his name was. A murmur of recognition swept through the bus as he came on board.

"*Guten morgen*," he began, with the trace of a smile. "Or perhaps I should say good morning, since all of you are familiar with English. It is a pleasure to greet each of you again."

He was more relaxed than Judith had seen him—friendlier, much less stiff and formal than before. Maybe it had to do with the fact that he was speaking to fifty people instead of one. Whatever the reason, Ehrlich went on.

"The time has come to proceed with our plan. As many of you are no doubt aware, you are all musicians. In the past, I have met with each of you

individually. Now you will be taken to Salzburg to
join with fifty of your contemporaries. In all, there
will be one hundred of you, gathered together from
all parts of the world for a single performance. In
Salzburg, you will be hosted by Herr Victor Pesage,
the person who has provided so generously for you
all. Feel free to discuss the project and its financial
rewards openly among yourselves. Enjoy these days.
They will be a marvelous adventure for you all.''

He paused, as though anticipating questions; then
backed off the bus when none were forthcoming. The
door closed. The driver turned his key in the ignition
and the journey began. Through Vienna, the outer
city and suburbs. After that, there was farmland,
with fields lying fallow for the coming winter. Still
anxious, Judith turned and began to talk with the
young man beside her.

"I'm an oboe player," he offered. "From Califor-
nia, just north of San Francisco. Can you believe
this? A trip to Europe, plus ten thousand dollars!"

The bus moved swiftly through the rolling hills of
Austria, past Amstetten and Linz. In the distance,
Judith could see the white peaks of the Alps shim-
mering in the sun. Maybe the murders were an aber-
ration, she told herself, perpetrated by someone other
than Klaus Ehrlich. Maybe Pesage would have them
play their concert and send them home. If only she
could get through the next three days alive and well,
she'd never complain or worry again. Think positive,
she decided. That was the solution. And positively
the first thing she planned to do when she got to

Salzburg was to call Marritt and tell him she was there.

"What did you think of your music?" asked the oboe player. "Mine was wonderful. I can't wait to hear it as a whole."

The bus drew closer to Salzburg. They went through the town, then out into the countryside again, past an old castle and farms. Finally, they came to a massive stone wall about nine feet high that ran along the highway to a wrought-iron gate. The bus stopped. A guard pulled the gate open, and they drove inside, up a private road maybe a hundred yards long. Judith looked out the window. Straight ahead was a mansion, four stories high, in one of the most incredible settings she'd ever seen. A rolling lawn seemed to go on forever, bordered by distant woods on either side. The grounds were green and neatly manicured, dotted with stone sculptures and the remains of flowers. The mansion itself was mostly stone, covered with heavy clinging vines, now devoid of leaves because of the season. Beyond the mansion, the lawn sloped gently to a clear blue lake with a slate terrace in between.

The bus came to a halt just short of the portico, and the driver signaled for his passengers to disembark. Simultaneously, the door to the mansion opened, and a stocky man in his mid-fifties appeared. He was about five-foot-six and powerfully built. He waited patiently as the musicians gathered. Then he spoke.

"Good afternoon. My name is Victor Pesage, and it is my pleasure to welcome you to my home. I am quite sincere when I say that it is an honor to be associated with you all." Drawing his audience closer, he continued. "A group of your contemporaries arrived earlier this morning. Today you will rest. Tomorrow we will rehearse twice for a total of six hours. The day after, we will perform. But come, before anything else, let me show you the grounds."

Pesage led; the others followed. Staying within the middle of the group, Judith tried to put her thoughts in order. "The mansion was built in 1764," she heard Pesage saying. "It predates the road by ninety years. For almost a century, visitors from town came by water rather than struggle through what was then a very deep forest."

He was rather handsome, she decided—not in a conventional sense, but with features that radiated artistry and emotion.

"You will be expected to remain on the mansion grounds at all times. It is, of course, too cold to go swimming, but I will warn you just the same. A great deal of barbed wire remains in the lake from World War Two. At that time, the mansion was used by the German High Command as its headquarters in Austria. It would be extremely foolish for any of you to go in the water."

One by one, Pesage pointed to stone sculptures and the lake terrace design. Put thoughts of murder aside, Judith realized, and the mansion was quite stunning. One hundred musicians were gathered together; and ninety-nine of them had to be ecstatic over their find.

"I have done everything possible to restore the former beauty of my home. Certain rooms have been preserved exactly as they were in the eighteenth century, although conveniences such as electricity and modern plumbing have been added on several floors. You may move freely throughout the mansion. Only my private study and personal living quarters are closed. You will share rooms during your stay, two of you in each room. A list of room assignments is posted inside the front door. Enjoy these days. They will be the finest of your lives."

It was mid-afternoon. Richard Marritt put down the telephone receiver and checked his watch for what seemed the thousandth time. He was going slightly crazy. Where was Judith Darr? For hours he'd been trying to find her, but she had simply vanished.

The hotel's records showed that her suite had been reserved in person, and paid for in cash. There was no place for him to look, nowhere to turn. All he could do was wait by the telephone and hope she called. Three times, he had asked the hotel desk if there was a message. Three times, they'd told him no. In all his life, Marritt had never felt more helpless and alone.

Judith would never have left on her own. That meant either she was being held captive, or the unthinkable had occurred. Maybe he should call Dema in New York. He hadn't eaten since morning, but it was imperative to stay in his room in case Judith called. He would review every clue, go over absolutely every detail. Four thousand miles from home, Richard Marritt was trapped, hoping desperately for a signal that would lead him to Judith Darr.

The mansion was incredible. She'd been there for four hours, and it was still difficult for Judith to believe what she saw. Each of the public rooms was like a museum, with paintings, tapestries, and glittering chandeliers. Even the corridors were magnificent, with Oriental rugs spread at intervals over polished marble floors.

Of all the rooms, the one called the Great Hall—a hundred feet long and fifty feet wide—was the most impressive. Centrally located on the second floor, it rose fifty feet to the roof of the mansion. An hour earlier, Judith had stood on one of two balconies overlooking the hall and stared down. Three huge chandeliers, magnificently assembled, sparkled and shone. The ceiling was covered with plaster ornamentation in a rococo style. The walls were adorned with tapestries and murals depicting Greek and Roman gods. Porcelain pieces were set around the room. And on the floor, one hundred chairs—each with a red velvet cushion and gilded wood frame—were arranged in the pattern of a symphony orchestra.

Otherwise, save for music stands and a podium facing the orchestra, the floor was bare.

One hundred musicians; one hundred chairs—a concert hall of unique proportions. Marritt had been right. Victor Pesage was planning to conduct a symphony orchestra. Judith continued on through the mansion, which was an endless stream of glitter and gold. But what she couldn't find was what she wanted most—a telephone.

Just before the dinner hour, Judith returned to her room on the third floor. In contrast to the mansion's public areas, it was sparse and small—not unlike a servant's quarters or college dorm. Two single beds were separated by a night table. There were two chairs, a closet, a sink, and a shower. The walls were cream-colored, the lighting consisted of a single light bulb. Her roommate was French, with an English vocabulary limited to orchestral terms.

A loud bell—the call for dinner—reverberated throughout the halls. Putting her thoughts aside for the moment, Judith joined her fellow musicians on the first floor. Like the Great Hall, the sixty-foot-long dining room, with its elaborate inlaid wooden floors, was extraordinary. Ten round tables were surrounded by heavily carved mahogany chairs, one hundred in all. An overhead chandelier reflected the light from a hundred candles. The walls were paneled with carved walnut, gilded with fourteen-carat gold. At one end of the room, a long buffet table was covered with platters of food—a feast that surpassed any Judith had ever seen. Damask draperies shielded

French doors. In many ways, it was like a scene from another era, two centuries before.

One by one, the musicians took plates and helped themselves to food and wine. From the rear of the room, Victor Pesage looked on. Judith saw him and tried to decipher what was in his eyes. Surrounded by the talent he had brought together—in a roomful of people who were beholden to his wealth, eating his food, living in his home—he seemed oblivious to them all. His face bespoke neither pain nor joy. It was a mask, giving no clue as to his true intentions. He was somewhere else. And then suddenly, instinctively, Judith knew what was happening. Victor Pesage was listening to music—music in his mind—music that would be played in the Great Hall tomorrow for the first time.

And then something else happened that sent chills running up and down her spine. In the light of the candles, from where she stood, it seemed that Victor Pesage looked exactly like Beethoven.

Chapter 26

BREAKFAST AT THE MANSION was a replay of dinner, with silver platters piled high in a buffet setting. Fresh fruit, bacon, sausages, and eggs; trays laden with croissants and strudel. After a night of turbulent sleep, Judith sat in the dining room, surrounded by her contemporaries, yet isolated and alone. All around her, there was excitement and anticipation. Just before nine, she went upstairs with her viola to the Great Hall. Most of the musicians were already there, tuning their instruments. The range of nationalities,

representing every cultural capital of the world, was
staggering. Judith checked the seating chart by the
door, and moved to her assigned chair. Precisely at
nine—the appointed hour—Victor Pesage entered the
hall.

In the light of day, he looked considerably less like
Beethoven. Still, the resemblance was there—the bil-
lowing hair, piercing eyes. And his hands. Judith
couldn't remember ever having seen a portrait of
Beethoven's hands, but she'd read about them. They
had been powerful, with thick veins and fingernails
cut short, strong.

All eyes were fixed on the conductor as he stepped
to the podium. "For the next three hours," he told
them, "I will demand your constant attention. We
will start with the first movement."

Judith buried herself in the music as the playing
began. Everyone in the room was a virtuoso performer. She was determined to play on a level as
high as anyone else, to blend perfectly with the other
violas and with the orchestra as a whole.

"Violins," she heard Pesage calling, "you must
vibrate more. And you must listen to each other.
Look at me, *please*!"

The "please" was a command, harsh and cold.
But, with satisfaction, Judith sensed that Pesage was
a competent conductor. He knew the score, his ability to communicate was more than adequate, and he
was pacing them well. Pacing—the gathering of musical peaks and valleys, inspiration, the natural talent
for conducting that could not be taught or learned.

"The strings are behind; you must attack together. At the fortieth measure, the melody isn't coming through. . . . Horns, after your crescendo, there is no break. Do it again—this time, properly." Judith watched him, sometimes peripherally, more often straight on. His expression ranged from flamboyant to stern. It shifted with changes in the music's tempo and mood.

A dazzling setting, a brilliant orchestra. And, above all, the music. It was awesome, unlike any symphony she'd ever heard: turbulent, swirling, cascading sounds; strong, vibrant, joyous, bold. At times, the emotional impact of what the orchestra was playing seemed on the verge of shattering them all. Yet, at each such moment, Pesage would lower his baton. He was teasing, not allowing them to hear the symphony or any single movement as a whole.

Starting, stopping, they worked their way through the first two movements. "You have done well," he told them. "We will stop now, and begin again this afternoon."

Richard Marritt looked at his watch. It was a few minutes before noon. He had been in the room for twenty-four hours. During that time he'd slept fitfully, watched television, and waited for a clue—any clue—concerning the whereabouts of Judith Darr. There was nothing. No telephone calls, no note, no flash of inspiration, no hint of where she'd gone. He

couldn't stand staying in the room much longer. He
had to get out and do something, however futile. But
what? How? Where should he begin? All he had was
the notion of a Tenth Symphony by Beethoven.

Desperate circumstances required grasping at straws.
Marritt went down to the lobby. The hotel gift shop
had two guidebooks on Vienna. He bought them
both, and went outside to a row of taxis by the hotel
door. The first two drivers didn't speak English.
Marritt settled on the third. Both guidebooks were
generous in their treatment of Beethoven. During his
thirty-five years in Vienna, they revealed, the composer had lived in thirty winter residences and as
many summer ones. Over time, only three of the
homes had been preserved.

"The Pasqualati House," Marritt told the driver.
"First District [and here he stumbled] at number
eight Moelkerbastai."

The driver lowered the flag on his meter and pulled
away from the curb. Oblivious to the sights, Marritt
studied his printed guide. The Pasqualati House had
been Beethoven's primary residence from 1804 through
1815. It was there, in 1814, that Anton Schindler had
visited the composer for the first time, carrying a
note to the master up four flights of stairs.

Ten minutes after the ride began, the cab pulled to
a halt outside an ancient five-story structure. Marritt
got out and told the driver to wait until he returned.
The detective strode up a rutted cobblestone walk.
He entered through an old wooden door, painted
brown; then climbed a stone spiral staircase, ominous

and dark, that rose to the fourth floor. A two-room flat, once the home of the world's greatest composer, had been converted into a small museum. A solitary guard stood at the door. With no real sense of what to look for, Marritt stepped inside. All he wanted was a clue, anything that would lead to Judith Darr.

The walls of the first room were covered with sketches and prints—a lithograph of Beethoven on his deathbed, photographs of the composer's last apartment and of his tomb, several oil portraits—eighteen items in all. Two glass-enclosed cases stood on the floor, each with music written in the composer's hand. A silver salt-and-pepper set, a lock of hair cut hours after Beethoven died. No clues. Try the next room. More portraits, a large clock once owned by Beethoven, a bust of the composer. In the center of the room was a piano, smooth and highly polished, with a clear plastic cover over the keys. Almost reverently, Marritt ran his hands along the body of the piano, then tugged at the cover. To his surprise, it was unlocked and lifted up, leaving the keys exposed.

Beethoven played this piano! His fingers touched these keys! The museum guard was out of sight. One note, Marritt told himself. That's all. Bending over, the detective fingered middle-C. A clear note sounded. Gently, he lowered the cover. He liked what had just happened. Richard Marritt—New York City cop—had played the same piano as Beethoven. Whatever followed, no one could ever take that away from him.

The Eroica House, in the 19th District at 92 Doeblinger Hauptstrasse, was the detective's next

stop. Beethoven had occupied two rooms on the
ground floor in 1803. Inside, another small museum
offered lithographs and memorabilia, but no clues.
The house where the Heiligenstadt Testament was
written—Number 6 Probusgasse—was third on the
detective's itinerary. Same result.

The afternoon was wearing on. Marritt was running out of places to go. Frantically, he racked his
mind for a puzzle piece that might fit. Museums were
useless. Given the fact that he didn't speak German,
the libraries of Vienna were off limits. What to do?
He wasn't sure what he was looking for but, suddenly, one place seemed where it was likely to be
found.

The afternoon rehearsal was going well. Judith
sensed complete commitment in the orchestra's sound.
And Victor Pesage was an even more skilled conductor than she had realized. He had taken a hundred
immensely talented musicians and given them room
to play, molded them into an orchestra capable of
producing extraordinary sounds. He had shaped the
music and captured the emotional content of the piece
against formidable odds. Beethoven's symphonies were
the most difficult in the world to conduct. They were
extremely complex, with so many pieces to fit together. *And the music was Beethoven.* Judith was
sure. People had tried to write like Beethoven before,
but all had failed. Works of genius defied imitation.

Beethoven had written this symphony—the one they were playing now.

Or playing as much of it as Pesage allowed. Like puppets on a string, he kept them dangling. The symphony had four movements, and he refused to let them play it as a whole. Even the movements were broken down.

"We will begin again at measure forty-five. Bass clarinet, you must play louder. Good. Let us go on. . . . Measure one-eighty-seven. The brass is too loud, all of you. I can't hear the strings. . . . Now you must attack the music. Fortissimo! Fortissimo! I know you are tired, but we will do it once more."

At five o'clock, the second rehearsal came to an end. The musicians left the hall in small groups. Judith remained behind in her chair, alone. Somehow she had to contact Marritt and tell him where she was. She had to find a telephone. Despite Victor Pesage's warning, she had to leave the mansion grounds.

Quietly, trying to go unnoticed, Judith left the Great Hall, walked downstairs, and slipped out the front door. There was no sense in crossing the lawn to the road. A hundred yards distant, she could see the wall, nine feet tall, stone. Better to head for the woods that bordered the property on either side. A half mile away, past hedges and the lawn, the forest's protective cover beckoned. Looking back to see if anyone was watching, she moved away from the mansion. Even if Pesage saw her, there would be no danger. After all, he had told them they were free to explore the grounds.

The woods were dark. The sun was setting. In the forest, branches and vines tugged at her arms. Resolutely, Judith pushed on. Forty yards. Fifty. Distance was growing hard to measure. A sudden drop in the ground—a hole dug by some kind of animal—caused her to stumble and fall. She got up and pressed on. Something huge loomed before her. She drew closer. It was the wall. The wall! It fronted the grounds along the road; it extended all the way around through the woods on either side. There was no way to climb over. But she had to get out. A thought struck her— she could follow the wall to the water and wade around until she reached the outside boundary of the wall. But no sooner had the thought come to mind than it was gone. "It is too cold for swimming," Pesage had told them, "but I will warn you just the same. A great deal of barbed wire remains in the lake from World War Two. The mansion was used as headquarters for the German High Command. It would be extremely foolish for any of you to go in the water."

They were prisoners, all of them; trapped behind barbed wire and a massive stone wall.

The Central Cemetery in Vienna was surrounded by a crumbling brick wall. In too many places, the mortar was chipped or gone. Richard Marritt made his way past antiquated tombstones. The trees were bare; the air, cold. An old, toothless woman approached, and stretched out her hand. She was short and heavy, wearing a baggy dress and tattered coat, with a basket of flowers slung over her arm.

"Zehn schillinge."

"I don't speak German."

"Zehn schillinge," she repeated, thrusting the basket toward him.

Marritt reached into his pocket and took out some change. Not bothering to count it, he dropped the money into the woman's palm. Bowing low, she handed him a flower.

Up ahead, a small grassy area was circled by conifer pines. Marritt stepped inside the enclosure, and looked around. Now that he was here, he wasn't sure what he expected to find. Five monuments stood their ground:

Wolfgang Amadeus Mozart
1756–1791

Johannes Brahms
1833–1897

Franz Schubert
1797–1828

Johann Strauss
1825–1899

Then a tall white slab of marble, with one word inscribed in coal black letters at the base:

BEETHOVEN

Beethoven. Beethoven! Frantically, the detective
racked his mind, but found no clue to lead him on.
Judith was gone, and he was at a loss as to how to
find her. The flower—a rose—was still in his hand.
The Pastoral Symphony was going through his mind—
the "Shepherd's Song" from the fifth movement,
from the first time he'd listened to Beethoven with
Judith Darr. Not sure he wanted to remember, the
detective threw the rose at the base of the tombstone,
then told the cab driver to take him home.

Back at the hotel, Marritt checked for messages.
Nothing. It was six o'clock. Weary and discouraged,
he went to his room. There really wasn't anything he
could do anymore. He'd tried it all, and for all his
efforts, he had failed. He should probably stay in
Vienna for two days more. Then, on November 9,
when the return flight to New York was scheduled—

The thought was interrupted by a knock on the
door.

"Yes?"

Again the knock.

"Who's there?"

"I have a message for Herr Marritt from Fräulein
Darr."

Thank God! From wherever she was, Judith had
found him. Somehow, she had managed; she had
found a way. Eager, anxious, Marritt flung open the
door. And then he knew that Judith might be alive,
but he was dead for sure. Because staring him right

in the face was a .32-caliber Sauer & Sohn automatic, and a voice was saying, "My name is Klaus Ehrlich. Please, you will step back slowly and raise your hands."

Chapter 27

HER HAND WAS SCRATCHED. There was a bruise on her thigh from the fall she had taken in the woods. Back in her room, Judith collected herself as best she could, then went downstairs to the dining hall. Near the entrance, a makeshift ensemble—two violinists, a cellist, and violist—was playing Brahms. Other musicians, conversing in groups of three and four, were talking about "The Symphony." Across the room, Victor Pesage was moving among the players, smiling, gesturing with his arms.

Judith approached the buffet table, plate in hand, alone. As she did, Pesage broke away from the others and came toward her.

"Good evening, Miss Darr. I trust everything is well."

Determined not to let her anxiety show, Judith smiled. "It's wonderful, thank you."

He had singled her out—or was it only her imagination? After all, he had been circulating, talking with the others. Maybe he was being a gracious host, that was all.

"I admire your talent, Miss Darr. Of all the musicians gathered in my home, you are among the most promising."

She wished the buffet line would move faster so she could get her food and be left alone.

"And I consider myself an excellent judge of talent, although I was not so gifted as you when I performed. Perhaps you know of my past at the Mozarteum in Salzburg."

"No, not at all."

"But, of course, there is no way you could know. I began as a violinist, but the faculty jury recommended that I rethink my career goals. I had the drive and ambition to be an excellent performer but the talent, I am afraid, was sadly lacking. Regardless, I had too much respect for the gifts of others to continue as a mediocre player, and one must accept those things in life that cannot be changed. So I decided to fulfill my needs and share my love of music as a patron of the arts in Vienna."

She had to say something to deflect suspicion. "Certainly, though, you're a very skilled conductor."

"Miss Darr, you are quite kind. From time to time, I have practiced the art, but I have always fallen short at the political aspects of the trade. Despite my wealth, I am rather clumsy at politics."

He was playing with her, waiting for her to say something more.

"Herr Pesage, I'm very curious. Has the music we're playing ever been performed?"

Now it was Pesage's turn to measure his words. "To my knowledge, it has never been performed by an orchestra, although I have heard it in my head many times. If I am walking in the hills, I hear the music. By the side of a lake, I hear its sound. It is always in my mind."

"Who wrote it?"

Just for a moment, his eyes hardened, as though challenging her right to make that demand. Then the smile, which had never left his lips, returned to his eyes. "That, Miss Darr, is a question to be answered soon. Later this evening, a notice will be posted, advising that full performance of the symphony is scheduled for tomorrow. After the performance—for which you will, of course, be in formal attire—authorship of the symphony will be revealed."

"It sounds like Beethoven."

"In some ways, yes. But as any child knows, Beethoven's symphonies number only nine."

"Are you sure?"

The smile was gone. "Miss Darr, I have lived my life in admiration of Beethoven. All of music exists in his shadow. I would prefer that you not jest at his memory in my home."

"I'm sorry. I didn't mean—"

"What you did and did not intend is irrelevant. I have built an orchestra, offered a setting, and put in your hands the most awesome music ever known. I have invited you to participate in a sacred mission, the fulfillment of a dream. But I warn you, Miss Darr, I am not a patient man. Be careful, lest you go too far."

"There is a time for everything, Herr Marritt. A time to reap, a time to sow, a time for laughter. Now, regrettably, the time has come for you to die."

Marritt lay face down on the floor of his room. His police revolver had been stripped from him and thrown aside. Klaus Ehrlich stood above him, gun in hand, savoring his prey.

"I have watched you and Miss Darr for some time. And I must confess, I was impressed by your determination. Under different circumstances, I might even have been amused."

Marritt waited. The taunting went on.

"No doubt, you are curious regarding the demise of three very talented musicians. I will tell you simply that it troubled me from the start to include Rebecca Morris in the plan. I did so because of a weakness for beauty, but I have never trusted beautiful women and, as a precaution, I met with her in late August for a second time. Much to my dismay, I learned that a breach of security had occurred. One of her contemporaries had purchased a bow for ten thousand dollars. She refused to identify the purchaser, referring to him only as 'he' and indicating that certain information had been exchanged. Accordingly, it became necessary to liquidate both Mr. Hollister and Mr. Swados as well as Miss Morris.''

"And Arnold Buxton?"

"You have surmised correctly the reasons for Herr Buxton's demise. His accident was arranged for security reasons after he declined our offer. In truth, the killings were a most unpleasant task, but one learns to tolerate that sort of inconvenience if properly compensated. And, by any standard, I have been compensated quite well.''

Ehrlich stopped talking. Turning his face slightly to the right, Marritt saw the shadow of a gun rise. "Why?"

"Why, Herr Marritt?"

"Why? What's behind it? The money, the orchestra. Why?"

"Those questions, I am afraid, must remain unanswered. Stand up, please.''

The end was coming. Shaking, Marritt rose, first to one knee, then to his feet. Ehrlich pointed to the door. "You will do exactly as I tell you. At the first sign of resistance, I will kill you. Go now, out into the corridor.''

They left the room; down the hall, through a double door to the service elevator. The German pressed a button by the sliding door and waited. The car came. He motioned Marritt on and pressed "12" for the top floor. The elevator door closed behind them. . . . Twenty seconds. . . . Thirty. . . . The car moved upward. Finally, it stopped and the door opened. Again, Ehrlich motioned with his weapon. . . . Down a corridor, up a gray metal stairway, through a long passageway. Past three huge boilers and a sign that read RAUCHVERBOTEN. At last, they came to a heavy metal door.

"Open it."

Marritt obeyed, then stepped out onto the hotel roof with Ehrlich close behind. All Vienna lay before them, city lights sparkling against the evening sky. A bitter wind whipped at the detective's face, muffling the clatter of fans from a ventilation shaft nearby.

Once again, Ehrlich was speaking: "Executing you in the hotel room would have been unwise. The hotel staff is quite efficient. Your body would have been discovered when the towels were changed and your bed turned down for the night. The airshaft, however, is a different matter. It will be several days before your body is found, and longer still before it is identified. Please, you will walk slowly, straight ahead. Walk to your grave as the Jews were made to walk at Auschwitz and Dachau."

Marritt moved slowly toward the ventilation shaft. Ten yards. . . . Five. . . . Ehrlich's gun nudged against the back of his skull.

"You must move more quickly, Herr Marritt. Hope is a wasteful emotion. Do not try to change the inevitab—"

Marritt exploded. Spinning to the right, he reached back with his right arm and locked Ehrlich's wrist in the crook of his elbow. His left hand came over, clamping down on the barrel of the gun; and suddenly, nothing in the world mattered except who had the gun. This wasn't police training and they weren't on gym mats; it wasn't refined fighting in any sense of the word. It was a no-holds-barred savage encounter, two bodies locked together, scrambling on the tar-surfaced roof, pebbles grinding at their skin. The gun spun loose. Both men dove for the chance to survive.

Marritt won.

Kneeling, they faced each other. Marritt had the gun. It was his turn.

"All right, fucker. I'm asking questions, and you're allowed no wrong answers. After one wrong answer, I shoot you in the leg. After the second wrong answer, you're gone. . . . What's your name?"

"Klaus Ehrlich."

Marritt fired.

A cry of pain pierced the cold night air.

"What's your name?"

A blotch of crimson began to spread down the German's thigh. Marritt tightened his grip on the trigger.

"Heiden. My name is Karl Heiden."

"Where's Judith Darr?"

"In Salzburg."

"Tell me more."

"In Salzburg, at the home of Victor Pesage. There is a mansion on a lake. During the Second World War, it was a headquarters for the German High Command. To the townspeople, the location is well-known."

"Keep going."

"There is an orchestra, and a symphony. Pesage plans to destroy the music tomorrow, after it is performed."

"Who wrote the music?"

Heiden lunged. Marritt fired.

The German was dead before he hit the ground. Then all was still, save for the whipping wind and the roar of ventilation fans from the shaft beyond.

Stepping back, Marritt looked down. A stream of blood flowed gently from Heiden's skull. No way did the detective want to deal with the authorities on this one now; not in Vienna, not when he planned on being in Salzburg within hours. Straining, he dragged the body across the pebble-and-tar roof to the shaft. Then digging in with his heels, he lifted Heiden's corpse up to the edge of the abyss and hurled it down.

Back in his room, Marritt examined himself in the bathroom mirror and cringed. The left side of his face was bruised and swollen. Patches of skin had been torn from his arms. Stripping off what was left of his clothes, he turned the bath water on full force, then lowered himself into the tub. The water stung. Maybe that meant it was cleansing his wounds. Minutes later he got out of the tub. Blood was still flowing. Crimson splotches reddened yellow towels; but the cuts were superficial; they'd clot on their own. The important thing now was to find Judith Darr. . . . Downstairs to the hotel desk: "How can I get to Salzburg?" the detective demanded.

"By train," the clerk told him, "if you leave now."

At midnight, the night's last train pulled out of Vienna's West Banhof station. Marritt sat in a glass-enclosed compartment, alone. Mustard-colored drapes partially obscured the window view. At 12:10, a conductor opened the compartment's sliding door, and the detective held out the price of a one-way ticket to Salzburg. The methodical click of train wheels sounded against the tracks below.

At 12:49, the train stopped at St. Polten.

At 1:30, Amstetten.

The scrapes and bruises on the detective's shoulders and arms were starting to burn. A porter came by, selling coffee—black, strong. "I'm old and tired," Marritt thought to himself. "All I want is to get out of this thing alive and go home."

This thing; whatever this thing was. So many questions were still unresolved. Why put together an orchestra to perform in secret? Maybe Heiden had answered that when he said Pesage planned to destroy the music when the performance was done. But why destroy the music? What purpose was there in such a wanton act? And beyond that, even if Pesage forced the musicians to relinquish their scores, they could piece the symphony together after they'd gone home. It might not be easy; the musicians would be scattered all over the world. But it could be done. And if the others were anything like Judith Darr, it would be done. Unless—

The train jerked, then began to move smoothly once more.

The musicians would be able to reconstruct the music. . . . The thought didn't want to come. The musicians would be able to reconstruct the music *if they were alive* when the concert was done.

At 2:13, the train stopped at Linz.

At 2:39, Wels.

Marritt looked down at his watch. Back in New York, it was 8:39 P.M. David and Jonathan would be getting ready for bed now. "With God as my witness, I'll never do anything like this again." In six months, his twenty years as a cop would be up. Marritt had just promised himself that in six months he was retiring.

The train was slow in leaving Wels. Once again, the detective tried to anticipate what was to come. Victor Pesage lived in a mansion on a lake, a mansion formerly used by the German High Command. But once Marritt found the mansion, what then?

Three o'clock. The train stopped at Attnang-Puchheim. The detective sat still, preparing to summon every physical and emotional resource at his com-

mand. The minutes dragged by. 3:30. . . . 3:45. . . .
At 4:00 A.M. the train pulled into Salzburg. Marritt
got off and looked down the long, narrow platform.
No cabs were waiting. It didn't matter; in a few
hours it would be dawn and then rush hour. Someone
would be able to guide him to Victor Pesage's mansion. Meanwhile, he had to conserve his strength for
the ordeal to come.

A solitary wood-slatted bench stood nearby. Ad-
justing his shoulder holster Richard Marritt sat and
waited for the dawn.

Chapter 28

THE MORNING WAS COLD. In fireplaces throughout the mansion, embers glowed. Judith stood on the balcony level of the library and looked down.

In many ways, the library was her favorite room in Pesage's home. It was gracefully shaped, symmetrical, self-contained, with no windows and only one door. It was soundproof, completely shut off from the rest of the world. And so much knowledge was locked within—Plato, Socrates, Shakespeare—the art and wisdom of the Western world.

Two levels of shelves were built into the walls.
Access to the balcony, which circumscribed the room,
was by a spiral staircase opposite the door. Most of
the books were in German, although some, like Shakespeare and Dickens, appeared in original form. There
was a large music section, and a special collection of
rare manuscripts behind sliding glass doors.

Standing on the balcony, Judith assessed what had
happened and what was going on. She'd given up
trying to contact Marritt. Today was the dress performance. Tomorrow, according to her plane ticket, she'd
be flying home. Pesage's outburst of anger the night
before had left her frightened and feeling very much
alone. She shouldn't have mentioned Beethoven, but
it was too late to rectify the error now. Don't think
about it, she decided. Concentrate on something else—
like the orchestra. Pesage seemed to respect its members, but only as performers. There was no warmth
or fondness; but that was his loss, not theirs. She
wasn't exactly fond of Pesage either.

But she loved his library. The bottom tier had 40
bookcases built into the walls, each one with 7 shelves.
The balcony level had 40 more. Juggling numbers in
her mind, Judith calculated that 560 shelves times 50
books per shelf equaled 28,000 volumes in all.

Oriental rugs were spread across the library's parquet floor. The ceiling was ornate, with gilded plaster similar to that in the other public rooms. There
was only one flaw. Directly above Judith, three air
vents had been cut into the wall—small aluminum-
framed openings that looked fairly new. The library

was probably insufferably hot in summer without any windows and only one door. Some kind of air-conditioning had been installed, but whoever installed it had cut away part of a gilded rococo swirl.

It was 10:00 A.M.; the dress performance wasn't until noon. That meant Judith had an hour to spare before she went back to her room and changed into her gown. Some fresh air would do her good. She could take a stroll around the mansion grounds. She'd walk to the lake and, if she had time, maybe—

She went downstairs to the front door. It wouldn't open. Judith wrestled with the lock, but it held firm. She tried it again, but it was no use. The door seemed irrevocably closed. . . . Next, the French doors in the dining room. Locked. . . . Back door; the same. . . . Maybe she could open a window. . . . They all opened, but there was no way past the wrought-iron gratings that fronted them all on the ground floor. The gratings were decorative, very pretty; effective at keeping intruders out. They were equally effective at keeping house guests in.

Without a word having been spoken, Judith Darr was now forbidden to go outdoors.

Richard Marritt stood at the wall. Finding his way by cab to the mansion grounds had been relatively simple. Scaling the wall was another matter. It was virtually impregnable, nine feet tall. The front gate was locked. There were no footholds, nothing to grasp onto, nothing to hold. Slowly he made his way along the barrier, looking for an opening, a place to climb. The wall curved away from the road, toward the lake. The detective followed it into the woods. He had to keep going, had to find a way to get over the wall. A large dogwood tree stood nearby. Marritt stopped. Ten feet above, a limb extended ever so close to the wall. It was worth a try.

Wrapping his arms and legs around the tree trunk, Marritt began to climb. Just a few feet off the ground was all he needed; enough to reach the branch that extended to the wall. Keep going. . . . Almost. . . . The rough bark of the trunk tore at the nascent scabs on his hands and arms, but he kept climbing toward the limb. Another foot up; six inches more—and he was there! Pulling hard, Marritt hoisted himself onto the limb, then slowly began making his way toward the wall. He had only a few more yards to go, but his weight was starting to bring the bough down almost level with the top of the wall. He couldn't go any farther, and he was four feet short of his goal. Four feet. There was only one way to do it—spring off the limb, go for the wall, and hope he made it.

Arms out, like a swimmer off the blocks at the sound of a starter's gun, Marritt dove for the wall. His hands clutched at a ridge of stone. His legs kicked air. Now his forearms were on the top of the wall. His weight was tearing at his shoulders and arms, but he was going to make it! In one final burst of exertion, Marritt pulled himself over the wall and burst dropped to the ground, exhausted, bleeding from all the places he'd bled the night before. But he was over the wall.

A few minutes before noon, Judith entered the Great Hall. Her black silk gown was simply fitted and flowing. Her slip rustled against the fabric as she walked. All around, orchestra members were wearing formal jackets and gowns comparable to her own. How incredibly eerie, she thought, to be all dressed up without an audience. They were dressed for the moment, for Pesage, and for themselves. And now that the moment had come, she was excited and scared. But more than anything, she wanted to hear the music now.

They'd rehearsed in the Great Hall twice previously, but somehow it seemed more magnificent today than before. An orchestra is a tool like no other for producing sound, but setting mattered. And the setting was superb—glittering crystal chandeliers, tapestries, murals, the inlaid marble floor. All one hundred musicians were in their chairs now, tuning their instruments. At precisely noon, Victor Pesage entered the hall. Judith stared. He was dressed in clothes styled two hundred years before: a blue frock coat with brass buttons, black knee breeches, silk stockings, an embroidered vest, shoes with bowknots. Under his arm was a symphony score, but it was a different copy from the one he'd used before. This one was on coarse paper, brown with age. It looked like an original, well over a century old.

Automatically, as they would for any conductor before a performance, the orchestra rose. Pesage stepped to the podium, gestured for them to sit, and opened the score:

"Good afternoon. I believe this to be the finest orchestra ever assembled. It is my honor to conduct you."

Then his arms flew up, his baton cut through the air, and the music began.

Slowly, Richard Marritt made his way through the woods to the edge of the lawn. The grounds were deserted. He'd never seen anything like them before. Statues, flower beds, neatly trimmed hedges in end-less rows. And right in the middle, a mansion, four stories tall. Now that he was here, though, he wasn't sure how to get in, short of walking up and knocking on the door. Overhead, the November sun shone directly down. Suddenly, a burst of music erupted from behind the mansion's walls.

Crossing the lawn, Marritt came to a side door. It was locked. He tried another entrance. The handle wouldn't turn. The patio was locked. Iron gratings covered the windows on the ground floor. Stepping back, the detective looked around. Heavy vines, form-ing a natural rope ladder, wound their way up the portico to the second floor. "Oh, Christ! Not after what I've been through so far."

Summoning the last vestiges of strength from his arms, Marritt began to climb. Five feet. . . . Ten. . . . Up toward the railing, along the vines, straining, pulling, with his legs, his shoulders, his body. Just a little more. Lift! Hold on! Over the railing; he was there; on the balcony above the portico. The balcony door was unlocked. Marritt turned the handle, and stepped inside into the corridor on the second floor.

An orchestra was playing. He could hear thunder reverberating through the halls. Mesmerized, he followed the sound, down a towering passageway to a double door. All that stood between him and a hundred musicians was the door. He would open it just a crack. Holding his breath, Marritt turned the handle. The door wouldn't budge. Leaning forward, he pushed harder. The door was locked; it held firm. And there was no way to tell whether Judith Darr was with the others inside.

Maybe the rest of the mansion would yield a clue. Drawing his revolver, Marritt made his way down the corridor. Like the grounds, the halls were deserted. Each room he came to was as magnificent as the one before: the walnut-paneled dining room; several sitting rooms, with towering ceilings, richly upholstered furniture, and ornate walls; a series of bedrooms; and, finally, a narrow stairway that led to a low-ceilinged corridor totally unpretentious, completely different, from what the detective had seen before.

Clutching his revolver, Marritt continued on. The corridor was dark. At the end was a heavy wooden door. Turning the knob, he pushed forward, and stepped into a small, dust-filled room. A kerosene lantern hung by the door with a box of matches nearby. The orchestra was only faintly audible. Lighting the lamp, Marritt looked around.

The room appeared to be a storage area. Boxes and canisters were piled high. The walls were bare, save for the lantern and an aluminum-framed portal on the far wall. The air was dank; the smell, familiar but, what it was, Marritt wasn't sure. Holding the lantern to one of the canisters, he searched for a label. There it was—Zyklon B.

Stepping back, Marritt shuddered. Zyklon B—a simple combination of carbon and nitrogen atoms with the odor of bitter almonds, also known as cyanide. He knew enough from his police training to have a vivid image of what befell cyanide victims. The amethyst blue crystals were harmless if smelled but, ingested or acid-activated, they were lethal. They shut down the body's energy-producing ability and blocked its capacity to deliver oxygen. Rapid breathing was followed by rising blood pressure. Within minutes, respiratory and heart functions stopped completely. A single gram was lethal dosage for five adults. And now, in Salzburg, Marritt had stumbled upon a remnant of Hitler's death machine, lying unattended in a centuries-old mansion once used by the German High Command. Closing the door behind him, Marritt left the room and continued on.

It was coming too fast. The orchestra couldn't possibly maintain the pace Pesage was demanding—but they could; they did. He knew their limits and was capable of extending them to that very point without going beyond. He stood before them, lifting notes with the tip of his baton; chopping, slashing; communicating with his body, his strokes, even his eyes. And the sound created was as gloriously awesome as any Judith Darr had ever heard. The music was Beethoven; she was sure. He had constructed a symphony with sounds that reached out across the universe. He was a God. And all the players were an Army of the Lord, led by a Commanding Angel after the fall.

Now the music was marching through time, a grand parade of all music Europe had known. Majestic, grand; combining moods so numerous that Judith was at a loss even to begin to understand. To do that, she'd have to hear the symphony so many more times; and even then, the meaning of this music would defy translation into words.

The final movement was nearing an end. She grieved for past generations to whom the music had been denied. She gave thanks for its presence in her life now. All of history was reverberating in the hall. Man's hopes and fears; happiness, pain, sadness, joy; falling in hammering, thunderous blows. The baton trembled in Pesage's upraised hands. The final note sounded, then died away, and all was still. For a moment, the musicians sat silent, stunned, not believing what they had heard. Then, as one, they rose and began to applaud. They applauded their surroundings, from the towering gilded ceilings to the polished marble floors. They applauded each other for their performance and shared bond. They applauded this strange man, who had brought them together only two days before. And above all, they applauded the music, whose origin they did not know. As the roar crescendoed, Pesage stood still. Then, almost imperceptibly, he bowed: "You have filled my home with beautiful music. I accept your gratitude as it is justly given—in praise of Beethoven."

Marritt was exhausted. He hadn't slept for thirty hours. His wounds were bleeding. His muscles burned. He wasn't even sure what he was looking for.

Except for the Great Hall, the rooms were deserted. Whatever servants Pesage employed had been dismissed for the afternoon. In one of the bedrooms, the detective found a silver pitcher filled with water. Lifting it to his lips, he drank thirstily, a trail of water streaming down his chin.

What time was it? 1:30 P.M. He'd been in the mansion for over an hour. How much longer would it be before he found what he wanted—or was, himself, discovered? He clutched his gun. Karl Heiden had been dispatched to kill him a day before. Too many people were dead for Marritt to let his guard down now.

His strength was ebbing. Yet he pressed on. Another bedroom revealed nothing. Next a lounge, with lots of chairs. Maybe he should sit, just for a minute; then he'd get up and start again. Wearily, Marritt lowered himself into a heavily carved mahogany chair. It felt good, almost seductive. But something was different; there was a change. And then he realized that the orchestra was no longer playing. The symphony was done.

Judith had experienced euphoria in her life, but never like this. And she'd probably never know anything like this again. They had played The Symphony. It was Beethoven. Years from now, centuries in the future, historians would recall this hour. There was so much to share, so many things to think about and say and do. But for the moment, she was content simply to stand in the library and watch what was going on.

The post-symphony reception was a lavish spectacle. The once-quiet library had been transformed. Tables normally used for reading were laden with caviar and champagne—so much caviar and so much champagne that Judith had trouble imagining the cost of it all. The music was still playing in her mind. She wanted to sing, or better still, to gather the orchestra together and play the symphony through a second time, and a third, over and over, until she was satiated. Maybe they could play it again tonight, if

Pesage was willing. He had to be. She'd watched his
face as they'd performed. She had witnessed a man
experiencing the most important moment of his life.
She had seen the exhaltation in his eyes as he led
them to the library, shut off from the rest of the
world, to bask in the glow of their holy triumph.
She'd find him and ask if he were willing to conduct
the symphony a second time. But looking around,
she didn't see him. Victor Pesage had left the room.
And even if Judith had seen him leave, she wouldn't
have known that he had bolted the heavy brass-
embellished door behind him.

Marritt's head throbbed; his entire body was tired
and worn. Resolutely, he pressed on. One floor below, the musicians had moved from the Great Hall to
another room. Maybe he should go down and con-
front them all, ask for silence, explain who he was
and why he had come. With his revolver still in
hand, Marritt moved down the corridor. How should
he begin? Maybe by putting away the gun; otherwise,
he'd scare the hell out of them all.

Footsteps sounded. Someone was coming up the
stairs from the floor below.

Marritt waited. Whoever it was had reached the
landing and was moving down the hall in the opposite direction. Gun still drawn, the detective followed, out of view, pursuing the sound—past a turn

in the corridor, up another flight of stairs. Then all was still.

Coming to a halt, Marritt looked around. Midway down the corridor, a heavy door was ajar. He moved to it carefully, peered inside the room, and saw a writing table, books, and several chairs. A large grandfather clock dominated the far wall. Beneath the mantelpiece, a fire burned. What mattered, though, was the short, stocky man standing by the fire, dressed in clothes Marritt had seen before only in picture books. And in his hands were sheets of coarse rough paper, brown with age, about to be thrown into the fire.

Marritt stepped into the room. "It's over. Stand still and keep your hands high."

Victor Pesage turned, but didn't answer.

"Let's go! Hands up! . . . Now move away from the fire."

Pesage took a step forward; then spoke in a calm, accepting manner. "You are to be congratulated, Herr Marritt. You are alive, and so I assume Karl Heiden is not."

"Where's Judith Darr?"

"Downstairs with the others. She's quite all right I assure you."

"Those papers; what are they?"

"Nothing that would interest a man of your limited intellectual stature."

Marritt tightened his trigger finger.

"They are man's greatest creation; nothing less, nothing more."

The detective waited. Almost compulsively, Pesage went on: "You were right, of course. We watched you rather carefully. At one point, we even tapped Miss Darr's telephone wire. It was Heiden who tracked the symphony down, starting with a letter at the Beethoven Museum in Bonn. Needless to say, the search was difficult. It required extensive financing, and Herr Heiden was interested in maximum compensation. Knowing of my wealth, he offered his findings to me rather than the museum board. When the manuscript was found, I paid a considerable sum."

"And then?"

"Then, Herr Marritt, I set out to fulfill a dream. My life has not always been a happy one. My talent was limited. Even as a patron of the arts, I was unable to succeed. In return for financial support, I asked only small favors—a woman's body now and then, dinner with whomever I chose. But the gifted musicians I sought to help seemed only to tolerate me for my wealth and made me the object of their humor. Therefore, I set out to construct an orchestra, the finest orchestra ever assembled, for the purpose of performing the greatest symphony created by man. I had hoped for a signal, a confirmation of purpose, across the ages from Beethoven. But none came. And I will confess, at times I fantasized that performing The Symphony would summon Beethoven from the grave."

"That's highly unlikely."

"I would agree."

Pesage moved forward. Marritt gestured with his

gun and the Austrian stopped, still holding the manuscript in his hand.

" Keep talking," Marritt ordered.

"Very well. What is it you would like to know?"

"Tell me about Heiden."

"Karl Heiden was a most efficient soldier. All that transpired occurred under his direction, with the help of several lower-level functionaries who were later disposed of. However—and here again I find myself in the act of confession—Herr Heiden and I had an unspoken mistrust for one another. From the beginning, I am convinced, he doubted my ability to conduct the orchestra. And I questioned his allegiance to the plan. You see, Herr Marritt, it was my intention to destroy The Symphony after it had been performed, to deprive the world of its glory, to live with the satisfaction that Beethoven's Tenth Symphony had been performed only once—under my command. However, I believe Herr Heiden loved music too much to accede to my desire. He would have kept The Symphony alive for the sake of posterity, and perhaps also to sell it to another buyer at another time. By disposing of him, you have done me a great service and spared me an exceedingly difficult task."

"And the musicians? Even without Heiden, they would have pieced the symphony together."

"That, Herr Marritt, would have been taken care of."

Then everything happened too quickly. Pesage stepped back and hurled the manuscript into the fire. Instinctively, Marritt reached forward to save it from

the flames; then pulled back, but it was too late.
Pesage had grabbed hold of an iron poker by the
fireplace, and brought it crashing down. Desperately,
the detective brought his left arm up to block the
blow, but it came too soon. A bolt of pain knocked
Marritt to the ground, his forearm shattered. He lay
there. Pesage fled from the room. Dazed, bleeding,
the detective staggered to his feet, groping for his
gun. Just beyond his reach, in the flames, Beethoven's manuscript was being consumed.

And then, in one terrifying moment, the ultimate
stage of Victor Pesage's plan was clear. Stumbling
forward, his left arm dangling uselessly at his side,
Marritt began to run. Through the corridor; down a
flight of stairs; gun in hand. Along another corridor;
up a narrow stairway toward the small dusty storage
room he'd been in before. As he neared it, he saw
that the heavy wooden door was open.

Marritt burst into the room. Victor Pesage was
standing by the far wall with a canister in his hand,
lifting it up, readying to pour. A thin stream of
activating acid traced its way through the aluminum-
framed portal into the library below. There was no
time for warnings, just time enough to fire one shot
that hit Pesage square in the back of the skull, spun
him around, and sent the canister's amethyst blue
crystals cascading harmlessly to the storage room
floor.

Afterword

MARRITT SAT IN THE COCKTAIL LOUNGE of the Intercontinental Hotel with Judith beside him. Except for the broken arm, his wounds were superficial. And the arm, set in a snow-white plaster cast, would heal with time. Tying up loose ends with the Austrian authorities had delayed going home by twenty-four hours, but that was all right. "Better late than never" was how the detective viewed the matter.

"What are you thinking?" Judith asked.

Marritt shrugged. "A lot of things. Mostly about

how someone new can enter your life when you least expect it; how ten weeks ago, I was worrying about delicatessens that sold beer on Sundays; how Victor Pesage probably thought you were privileged to die in the manner he had planned.''

A waitress came by, and Marritt looked at his watch. One more drink, and then it would be time to turn in for the night. Ten hours of sleep seemed about right.

"What about you?" he asked Judith. "What are you thinking?"

"I was wondering if we were going to bed together tonight."

She waited, measuring the effect of her words, then went on. "We've been leading up to it for a long time; you know that. We'd have gone to bed after the concert at Lincoln Center if it hadn't been for Ehrlich's letter. I know you're married; I'm not asking for an ongoing relationship; just a one-night celebration of our coming out of this whole crazy thing alive."

Reaching out, she touched the detective's hand. Somehow, the idea seemed very right to Marritt; four thousand miles from home; just this one time. When was it that Judith had first touched him? The night she'd given him her viola and put her hand on top of his; when she had taught him to make a musical sound.

Weighing his emotions, Marritt took a long look into her eyes.

"I don't know," he heard himself answer. "I'd

like to. I've thought about it a lot, probably a lot more than you have. It's just—'' His voice trailed off, then picked up again:

"Judith, for a long time I've been fighting the feelings I have for you. I know this sounds silly, coming from someone eighteen years older than you are, but in a lot of ways I'm confused. Sometimes I'm confused about my job. Other times I'm confused about my marriage. But there's one thing I'm sure of—going to bed together wouldn't make either of us any happier. I'd like to; it would be wonderful. But there's a lot about growing older that you don't understand; about spending time alone and wondering if you'll ever find someone you can trust and be close to, and then finding that person the way I did twelve years ago. The thing I'm proudest of, what makes my life worthwhile, is my wife and children. Sometimes, with all that goes on, I lose sight of that; but they're there, and if I'm lucky they always will be. For a couple of months now, I've been your protector; but that's really all I am or ever could be to you.''

"That sounds like a rejection.''

Reaching out, the detective touched her cheek with the palm of his hand. "I like you. You've given me something very special to hold onto. From now on, whenever I hear Beethoven, I'll think of you as my friend.''

"You're a nice man.''

"You're nice too.''

"And I owe you my life. How do I repay you?''

Marritt smiled. "I'll tell you what—and I'm serious about this. How would you like to give viola lessons to David and Jonathan? It wouldn't hurt for them to have a little culture."

"Richard, I'd love to."

"Good. And there's one thing more. The next time some guy with a German accent comes along and offers you ten thousand dollars to play a concert in Europe, promise me you'll tell him no."

"I promise."

"Thank you. And now, since we're on the subject of music, I've been waiting all day for a blow-by-blow account of Beethoven's Tenth. Is it any good?"

"It's incredible."

"What's it like?"

"Well, the first movement begins with something I've never heard in a symphony before. You see, in the traditional symphonic mode . . . ."

BESTSELLING BOOKS FROM TOR

☐ 58725-1 *Gardens of Stone* by Nicholas Proffitt $3.95
   58726-X   Canada $4.50

☐ 51650-8 *Incarnate* by Ramsey Campbell $3.95
   51651-6   Canada $4.50

☐ 51050-X *Kahawa* by Donald E. Westlake $3.95
   51051-8   Canada $4.50

☐ 52750-X *A Manhattan Ghost Story* by T.M. Wright
                                                     $3.95
   52751-8   Canada $4.50

☐ 52191-9 *Ikon* by Graham Masterton $3.95
   52192-7   Canada $4.50

☐ 54550-8 *Prince Ombra* by Roderick MacLeish $3.50
   54551-6   Canada $3.95

☐ 50284-1 *The Vietnam Legacy* by Brian Freemantle
                                                      $3.50
   50285-X   Canada $3.95

☐ 50487-9 *Siskiyou* by Richard Hoyt $3.50
   50488-7   Canada $3.95

Buy them at your local bookstore or use this handy coupon:
Clip and mail this page with your order

TOR BOOKS—Reader Service Dept.
P.O. Box 690, Rockville Centre,·N.Y. 11571

Please send me the book(s) I have checked above. I am enclosing
$_____ (please add $1.00 to cover postage and handling).
Send check or money order only—no cash or C.O.D.'s.

Mr./Mrs./Miss _____

Address _____.

City _____ State/Zip _____

Please allow six weeks for delivery. Prices subject to change without
notice.

MORE BESTSELLERS FROM TOR

GRAHAM MASTERTON

☐ 52195-1 CONDOR $3.50
52196-X Canada $3.95

☐ 52191-9 IKON $3.95
52192-7 Canada $4.50

☐ 52193-5 THE PARIAH $3.50
52194-3 Canada $3.95

☐ 52189-7 SOLITAIRE $3.95
52190-0 Canada $4.50

☐ 48067-9 THE SPHINX $2.95

☐ 48061-X TENGU $3.50

☐ 48042-3 THE WELLS OF HELL $2.95

☐ 52199-4 PICTURE OF EVIL $3.95
52200-1 Canada $4.95

Ramsey Campbell